BIRDIES

&

MAUI

HEAT

A Roc Reese Mystery

BIRDIES

&

MAUI

HEAT

A Roc Reese Mystery

DUKE CHARLES

For information about this title or to order other books and/or electronic media, contact the publisher:

Bethel 1808

Lewisville, TX 75057

DukeCharles.com

DukeCharlesWriter@gmail.com

ISBNs for Birdies & Maui Heat

Softcover: 978-1-947201-38-5
eBook: 978-1-947201-39-2

Printed in the United States of America

Dedication

To my daughter, Lisa,
my son, Brett,
and my son, Brad,
to my grandson, Stewart, (U.S. Navy),
my grandson, Aksel,
and my granddaughter, Lauren,
and to my two great-grandchildren,
Eleazar Gideon and Jaea Elizabeth,

I love you all,
Greatdaddygrandpa Duke

Acknowledgement

Many thanks to my bride, Corinne, for putting up with my nonsense for the last 150 years and making me the man I am today.

Very truly,
Duke

Table of Contents

Prologue   3

Front Nine

Hole 1   Reading the Greens   7
Hole 2   Let the Big Dog Eat   9
Hole 3   In the Rough   13
Hole 4   Laying Up   29
Hole 5   Saving Par   41
Hole 6   From the Tips   77
Hole 7   Slice   99
Hole 8   Pitch and Run   115
Hole 9   Roll It and Hole It   135

Back Nine

Hole 10 Grip It and Rip It   147
Hole 11 Blind Hole   161
Hole 12 Hole-in-One   169
Epilogue   171

Prologue

Lucy and I had been back from New Orleans for going on seven weeks, and she assured me that if I ever went back, it would be alone, or at the very least, with someone besides her.

My bites, scratches, and gunshot wounds had pretty much healed, and my golf game was back on track, and Crown Royal Reserve tasted good again as it should. We were back to kayaking and exercising, and Lucy's body was hard, tan, and utterly amazing, not that it was ever any other way.

My cell phone was sitting on the small table on my patio beside a tall Crown on the rocks, and I was watching the San Diego sun go down. Lucy was running some errands, and I was daydreaming about something as the ringtone from my cell jarred me back to real time,

"Hey, Roc! It's Trae; what's up, old friend?"

Trae Biggs ran a Learjet charter service out of Las Vegas and was indebted to me for keeping his ex-boss, Lyle Byrum, out of prison some months back before he was murdered down on Mustang Island on the Texas Riviera.

"Just living the good life, how about you my young friend?"

"Hey, Roc, I have a charter scheduled with nine filthy-rich guys here in Vegas going to Hawaii to play golf for a week or so, and I have three empty seats if you'd like to tag along? It'll be no charge, of course."

"Sounds like the perfect place to pursue our trade! I need to clear it with Lucy and JJ, but I'm gonna say, *hell yeah!* I can let ya know for sure in a couple of hours."

"Not a problem, and I can make your hotel, car reservations, and tee times from this end, and I'll add your airfare to the old geezers' bill."

"You're a prince among men, my young friend, *Mele Kalikimaka.*"

"Huh?"

"*It's the thing to say on a bright Hawaiian Christmas day*; should be just about Christmas as near as I can tell."

"Yes, sir, and we're leaving on the 20th."

"Sounds great to me! I'll be in touch."

"That's great, Roc. Looking forward to seeing you again!"

"You too kiddo."

I ended the call with Trae at the same time Lucy came in,

"Hey, Lucy-girl, get all your rat-killin done?"

"Yeah...I think so."

"Let me ask you a question..."

"Sure, what is it?"

"Would you mind if I went on a short business trip?"

"How short?"

"I don't know, seven, maybe, eight days."

"When?"

"In a few weeks."

"That's over Christmas, right?" her eyes started to narrow.

"Yeah, probably."

"Where?" she asked quietly with a hint of suspicion in her voice.

"Hawaii."

KABOOM! The bomb exploded,

"You want to go to Hawaii over Christmas without me?"

"Well, yeah, but only if it's ok with you."

I love messing with her mind.

"Rockland Reese, you old bastard! Have you lost your mind? Do you really think you can go to paradise and leave me here all alone?"

"Well...that's one way to look at it."

Hole 1

We took off from a private hangar at San Diego International Airport at 9am on December 20th. Lucy had finally forgiven me, and she looked fantastic: all tan and buffed and well, you know. I'll admit, I may have pushed the "messing with her mind" thing a little farther than I needed to.

On the plane, JJ was already snoring, and Lucy was in the restroom. I was helping the extremely beautiful hostess pour more than the normal amount of Crown Royal Reserve into an oversized glass with ice that I had found under the galley cabinet but only so she wouldn't have to make another trip to wait on me before she finished taking care of all the old geezers. I was sure she appreciated the thought, and I appreciated the view.

The flight time was approximately four hours and fifty-six minutes with nothing to look at but our gorgeous hostess while she brought me booze as I drank it, and of course, Lucy, and I were looking forward to several days of golf on some of the most beautiful courses in the world.

Life just couldn't get any better; but of course, it was all about to go south.

Hole 2

Three very large limos and a 15-passenger SUV to haul our luggage and golf stuff awaited us at the private hangar of the smaller of the two airports on the beautiful island of Maui.

The ride to the Ritz Carlton Kapalua was only about 17 minutes, and our room was a private villa on the beach with a full gourmet kitchen, two bedrooms and three bathrooms, a huge sitting room with a 100-inch, flat-screen TV and sound system, and all the whistles and bells, and there was a full-sized pool table, a fully stocked bar, and a private pool on our lanai, all that for only $4,700 and some change a night plus tax. JJ shared our villa because I needed a drinking companion after Lucy hit the sack at night.

Some folks might say that I have a drinking problem. It's not true; I thoroughly enjoy drinking and have since I was about six months into my four years in the Coast Guard. In fact, the main reason I left the service was because they wanted me to stay sober during working hours, and I wanted to stop working during my drinking hours, not exactly a match made in heaven and besides, what made them think I needed to be sober to cook the kind of crap they served to our sailors back in those days, anyways?

The beautiful hotel and golf course was built in 1997 on 22,000 or so, acres of pristine island property; the only problem was there were over 900 ancient burial sites (called *Honokohau*) underneath the pristineness, so of course, they were preserved. The Plantation Course, one of two on the property, was the home of the Hyundai Tournament of Champions. It was the first pro event of the year, and the condition of the course was second to none.

I had introduced myself to all nine of our traveling companions during our flight across the Pacific, and as it turned out, all but one knew me by my reputation, and of course, Lucy already had her own fan club onboard.

We were immediately invited to join their games, and the guy in charge added our names to the roster and told us that we may not be able to play together all the time because everyone was already putting in requests to be in Ms. Lucy's foursome, not that I blamed them. Her golf wear alone was worth the price of admission, which by the way, was $500 a round in advance, each, in cash, not counting the special events like *skins, birdies, greenies, closest to the pin,* etcetera, to be paid after each round. It sounded exactly like our kind of game!

The last time I was in Maui was the year 1976 while I was still in the military (the U.S. Coast Guard for those of you who haven't read about any of my other escapades or adventures) and damn, had things changed!

Hole 3

Day 1

At seven in the morning, breakfast was served at the clubhouse, and the buffet was amazing. A person could get any kind of fresh fruit imagined. There were juices that I had never heard of like the leya-leya-mua juice that was guaranteed to make your pecker stand at attention on demand at least three times a day, and well, you know I had to try it, and I had two large glasses just to make sure.

A person could also get absolutely any kind of breakfast fare imaginable, and the chefs challenged guests to order something that wasn't already on the menu, and I don't believe they've been stumped from conception to this day.

10am

We played the senior tees so far forward
that JJ and I could have literally thrown the
ball down the hill to the green on some of the
holes, and Lucy was on the ladies' tees ahead
of us. It was all she could do to keep from
laughing out loud. Somehow the old coots paid
off the pro, and we were allowed to play two
sixsomes

I hate playing slow; it's difficult for me to
stay focused, and my game can turn to crap
very quickly if I'm not careful; fortunately,
there wasn't a single person in the group who
could get within 20 shots of me with the
exception of JJ and Lucy, so I didn't have to
concentrate very hard. What should have taken
us about three-and-a-half hours to play, took
almost that long to make the turn.

We had decided to put all our winnings in a
pot and split it three ways. The first day, we
split $6,000 plus another $4,200 in special-
event cash, pretty much the way I saw it
playing out; not a single one of those old guys
belonged on a golf course of that caliber, or
maybe not a golf course of any caliber, but far
be it from me to speak my mind. I was just an
invited guest, and they didn't seem to mind
losing. I guess Lucy's *companionship* took the

sting out of it, or they all had so much money that it was just pocket change to them, who knew?

Day 2

The next day went pretty much the same way except that we had to play foursomes. JJ and I were on a different team; we had discussed that contingency and agreed that Lucy's team would win, and we stayed in the loop via cell phone, and I couldn't remember ever playing that bad.

JJ and I consumed an exceptionally large amount of Crown Royal and still had to throw off big time to keep from beating her team.

That evening after dinner, we sat on our lanai and put another $10,00 in the kitty, and I confessed,

"Guys...I just can't do this another day; my game could go completely south if I have to keep throwing off this hard."

Fortunately, Lucy and JJ agreed with me, and we decided to beg off the next morning and try to find another game or play on our own.

Day 3

I was up and out of the room at seven in the morning and walked over to the clubhouse but something seemed out of sorts as there were no maintenance people or grounds keepers working or even kitchen help hanging around the back door of the galley on their smoke breaks.

When I turned the corner from the flora and fauna-covered path, I saw why: everyone was standing around on the grass, staring towards the circular cobblestone drive in front of the clubhouse. An ambulance, a fire truck, and two police units all had their lights flashing, and most importantly, there was a body lying on the stone drive covered with a red blanket. I thought to myself,

That's not good.

I started to walk on by and head for the front door when one of the young assistant pros came up to me,

"Sorry about your friend, Mr. Reese."

"What are you talking about, Rick?" I asked.

"They found Mr. Morgan (the oldest and richest fellow on the junket) about 4:30 this morning when one of the cooks came to open up."

Charlie Morgan grew up in Japan; he was a military brat in the mid to late 50s and was pretty much a loner. He roamed the streets of Yokosuka and studied manufacturing techniques, watching the production of musical instruments, and he began designing them, which led to other successful products and eventually, computers, and he had billions of dollars rattling around in those deep pockets.

I turned to go back towards the police to see if I could be of any help.

"Thanks, Rick," I said as I backtracked.

I found a plainclothes cop who looked as though he might be in charge,

"Excuse me, officer..."

"Yes? What can I do for you, sir?"

"My name is Rockland Reese, and that gentleman was part of our group who all came over on a charter from the mainland."

"Mr. Reese..."

"Please, call me, Roc."

"Ok, Roc, I'm Lieutenant Pau of the HSP (Hawaiian State Police), but you can call me, Mongo."

"Mongo, as in *Mongo* from the movie *Blazing Saddles,* starring Alex Karras?"

"Exactly! My mother was a huge fan of football and the big screen and still is."

"One of my all-time favorites as well," I said, and I thought he did kind of resemble the character with his bulging biceps and all.

"Mongo, what can you tell me about the crime scene?"

"It looks like a plain case of robbery that went wrong, like he tried to resist and fell down or was pushed and possibly hit his head on the rock driveway."

I uncovered Charlie's head and saw a lot of trauma.

"I get the feeling that the assailant was young and inexperienced; most pros are well-aware that very wealthy people carry very little cash, just enough for tips and stuff; otherwise, they'd have to carry around a knapsack full of $100 bills, (everything else is paid for with unlimited black credit cards) and now, whoever did it is looking at a murder charge. Or perhaps it was a professional hit; his head did have quite a bit more damage than just a fall should cause."

Mongo replied as he turned, and he squinted his eyes as he stared at me,

"Yeah, Roc, that sounds about right," as he tried to figure me out.

"Can you tell me anything else about the crime scene, Mongo?"

"Not at the moment, Roc, but I'll definitely keep you in the loop as we find out more."

"I'm going to grab a cup of joe if you'd like to join me," I said.

"I could really go for a cup; give me a couple of minutes to check out a few things here, and I'll join you."

I walked into the dining room at the hotel and helped myself to a large, very expensive coffee mug and filled it from the giant, silver, coffee urn that was sitting on a beautifully hand-carved console that was about 20-feet long with a natural rock top unlike anything I had ever seen.

There were other containers full of all the expected fruit juices, including my new favorite, leya-leya-mau, and I couldn't say for sure that the juice lived up to its reputation or whether it was just the atmosphere, but life was pretty damn good with the exception of poor Charlie Morgan.

I was sitting and looking at the morning sun reflecting off of the beautiful Pacific Ocean when Lieutenant Mongo came up beside me with a mug of steaming coffee in one hand and his cell phone in the other. I motioned for him to sit, and he nodded as he spoke to someone on the other end.

"Hey, Roc, we've been trying to contact Mr. Morgan's next of kin, but apparently, he's a widower, and so we're trying to run down some other family members to notify."

"Wish I could be of more help, Mongo, but I just met him on the flight over."

"What do you know about the rest of the party?"

"Pretty much the same, except for my partners, Lucy Barnes and Jerry Johnson."

"Partners? What is it that you do?"

"We play golf."

"Golf? Like on the pro tour?"

"Kind of, except we play private matches with wealthy clients."

"So, you're hustlers?"

I cringed as it was not how I like to be described,

"Well, not exactly. We always give our marks, I mean, opponents (I smiled) a fair game, and they usually wind up beating themselves. Golfers are funny people: almost all of the amateurs consider themselves to be way better than they really are."

"So you are a pro?"

"Only in so much as I have never done anything but play golf for a living but never played the tour. Do you play?"

"No. Never had the time or money to spend to learn the game. So, these guys around the shop here could go play and get rich?"

"There are *golf pros* and *professional golfers,* and never the twain shall meet."

"I'm not sure I understand. I don't normally hang with this crowd; I'm more of a 'roast a pig on the beach on the weekend' type of guy," he responded.

"Rich folks are not so different. They think they are, but it's all in their minds, and golf pros are schooled to teach the game and run facilities and handle the business end of the game. Professional golfers, on the other hand, are the ones you see on TV who travel the world, play tournaments, and make boatloads of cash if they're good enough."

"So, you are saying that golf pros can't play?"

"Not necessarily, but for the most part, they don't have time to take their game to the level it needs to be to compete with the best in the world although there have been a few club pros who have made it to the big show over the years, but not so much these days. Most of the stars of the game are prodigies and start out training and playing from the time they are very young and don't do anything else except go to school, of course. Tiger Woods, for instance, was on TV when he could barely walk doing exhibitions; he was a prodigy, just like in music or science. By the time kids are 12 or 13 or even younger, someone has seen something very special in them and has started formally training them."

"Very interesting. I guess I never paid that much attention to the game. I always thought it was just a bunch of rich folks coming to the Islands to soak up the sun and throw money at the locals, so they would cater to them."

"Yeah, it's crazy; golf is the number one game in the world, so many people play *at* it, and that's what makes the pro tour so successful. All those billions of players can relate to them and actually think that one day they might quit work and go play pro golf or retire and go play the senior tour. Pipe dreams!"

I switched gears, "So, Mongo, what's the feeling in your gut about poor ol' Charlie?"

"Well, I've been thinking about what you said about rich folks, and we actually have very little crime around the resorts for that very reason, so this may go a lot deeper than that."

Mongo was a very friendly sort, but I got the impression he was still feeling me out, and I guess rightfully so as he really didn't know me from Adam."

Lucy walked up behind me and kissed me on the top of my head, and I thought Mongo was going to spit hot coffee all over himself. His eyes got as big as a 50-dollar golden eagles.

"Mongo, this is my partner, Lucy Barnes. Lucy, this is Lieutenant Pau."

The policeman jumped to his feet and shook her hand and held it for a couple of seconds longer than necessary,

"Please, call me, *Mongo*. It's my pleasure to meet you, Ms. Barnes."

"The pleasure is mine, Lieutenant...*Mongo*...is it? Like the movie?" she asked. "Daddy, didn't we just watch a western with a character named *Mongo?"*

"Yes, love, we did...the comedy *Blazing Saddles* a few months back."

"Yes, Ms. Barnes, my mother is a huge fan of that movie."

"How interesting!" and she left it at that.

"Can I get you a cup of coffee, my love?" I asked.

"Sure! I'd love one and a small glass of the *special* juice, if you don't mind," and she smiled.

I jumped up and headed toward my appointed tasks.

"You seem like a little more than just business partners, Ms. Barnes," Mongo observed.

"Please, call me, Lucy. Well...we were pretty close friends before we went into business together, and fortunately, we have stayed friends since."

"So, what is your role in the partnership?" Mongo asked with great curiosity in his voice.

"I play golf, just like Roc and JJ."

"That's very interesting. I guess I have been missing a lot and need to start paying more attention," and a large grin came across Mongo's dark, sun-scorched face.

Lucy looked him in the eye and gave him one of her beautiful smiles in return,

"Why, Lieutenant Mongo...are you flirting with me?"

"Well, ma'am, I believe I may be. I think it would be impossible for a normal man not to. No offence, I hope?"

"Not at all, Mongo."

"What have I missed?" I asked as I set Lucy's coffee and a juice glass of leya-leya-mau in front of her.

Mongo smiled when he saw the juice.

"Not a thing, love; we were just getting to know each other."

A waiter came to take our order, and I convinced Mongo to stay and join us. We dined on giant, ranch, fresh eggs, three to a plate. They brought a heated platter of breakfast meat, bacon, ham, several kinds of sausage, various types of potatoes, and they cooked the toast selections at our table. The food and the service was impeccable, and Mongo was overwhelmed as he had never dined like that before.

"What do you suppose the chicken looks like that lays these eggs?" Mongo asked, and we all laughed.

People were starting to fill the clubhouse for breakfast, and I pointed out the group of rich, old businessmen who we were associated with although they were pretty hard to miss as they mostly wore a look of shock and disbelief on their faces.

Mongo excused himself and walked over and introduced himself to the group of eight very successful looking old men huddled in conversation.

"So, Roc, what do you think is going on here?" Lucy asked just as JJ came walking up to our table.

"Hey...JJ...how about some breakfast?" I asked.

"I think I'm just gonna go with coffee and some of that magic juice that y'all stayed up *talking* about most of the night."

"Did we keep you awake? So sorry!" Lucy said with a grin. "I thought the walls were thicker than that."

"They are. I had to put my ear to a water glass against the wall to be able to hear anything at all!" and we all laughed.

"Lots of excitement here this morning, huh, pard?" JJ asked.

"Yeah...someone punched Charlie Morgan's ticket, and I'm not completely sure it was just a simple robbery."

"What do ya mean, love?" Lucy asked in surprise.

"Well, I guess it could have been one of the resort staff, and if it was, the police will run the suspect down in no time, but I have the feeling that it's quite a bit more complicated than that. One of the richest men in the world gets mugged on the hotel property at the time of night that most people his age have been in bed for five or six hours? Something just doesn't add up."

JJ jumped in, "This isn't going to be another one of those New Orleans' debacles is it? Because if it is, I'm going to catch the next plane home. I don't like being shot at and blown all to hell!"

"If it looks like it's going to get crazy, I'll give you plenty of warning, but they haven't asked me for any help at this point, and I didn't volunteer my services. Why don't you see if you can find us a game this morning?"

"Absolutely!" and JJ got up and headed for the pro shop, while Lucy and I finished our coffee and watched the amazing Hawaiian sun get higher in the clear, blue sky.

JJ returned about 20 minutes later,

"Hey, I found a couple of guys who think they're unbeatable and want a game. We're going to another course just up the road a few miles in about 45 minutes; they'll have a car outside the pro shop when we're ready."

"What's the game?" I asked.

"I don't know, but we're all playing scratch, and they look like they have some bucks!"

Hole 4

Larry, Gary, and the three of us stood on the first tee of an absolutely beautiful private course and discussed our bets; we left the particulars of the game up to them, so we wouldn't seem to anxious. As it turned out, those two thought they had found the motherload: two old guys and a lady who wanted to play for cash?

They suggested $200, two-down autos and wanted to wheel the three of us, which meant the two of them would play JJ and I as a team, JJ and Lucy as a team, and me and Lucy as a team.

We played two holes, and all three teams were square, and of course, Larry and Gary couldn't keep their eyes off of Lucy as she teed off from the ladies' box up ahead of us on every hole.

"What about greenies?" one of them yelled as we drove up to the third tee box, a Par 3,

"Say, a $100?"

"No problem!" JJ said in response.

Our new friends still had the honors since there was no blood, but I knew things were about to change.

They both hit good shots and were in birdie range. JJ and I had birdie putts just outside of them, and then it was Lucy's turn, and our opponents were licking their lips.

Lucy's shot was about 132 yards from her tee box to the pin; she bent over and teed up her ball, a glorious site by the way. She took an eight-iron and hit the ball very high, and it landed like a squirrel with sore feet, bounced once, hit the pin solid, and jumped back to settle about two-and-a-half feet from the hole.

Three skins, a birdie, and a greenie, when the two golf hustlers both missed their birdie putts, we could see the confidence drain from their faces, and when I made my birdie putt to beat them all three-ways, I knew they were finished, and they were, not another smile from either of them for the rest of the round.

"Who are you guys?" Larry asked.

"Whaddya mean?" JJ asked. "We didn't do anything special (the three of us were all over par by a stroke or two). You guys are just having a bad day."

And they did, they each lost over $3,500, and you would have thought they had lost the farm, and we (the three of us) got to play our game on an incredibly beautiful golf course.

When we arrived back at our bungalow, Mongo was sitting in one of the very comfortable chairs on our Lanai, almost dozing.

"Good afternoon, folks; how was your day?"

"Not too bad," I said. "Almost made enough to pay for the room tonight...almost."

"Wow! Sounds like you did well!"

"Could have been better, but our opponents ran out of cash. What can I do for you, Mongo?" I asked as we entered our room.

"We're going to indulge in a cocktail; will you join us?"

"Actually, I will. I'm off duty for a while at least, and I wanted to invite the three of you to a luau at the ranch this evening. I think you'll enjoy it, and I know the family will enjoy Ms. Lucy."

I poured four glasses of Crown Royal Reserve over ice and handed one to our guest, one to Lucy, and one to JJ, and we toasted.

I called the concierge, and he had a new, burgundy-colored, Mercedes S550 or whatever, the big one anyway, ready for us, and we headed north from the resort to the Pau Ranch following Mongo's directions. Fortunately, the ranch was exactly where Mongo said it would be, and we topped the hill to a view of Texas beef grazing and pineapples growing all with the deep-blue Pacific as a backdrop. The site was absolutely gorgeous!

We met Mongo's parents, grandparents, aunts, uncles, and cousins, and we didn't ask, but I guessed there wasn't a Mrs. Mongo. However, I assumed we'd find out soon enough.

There were a dozen or more kids playing in the ocean and laughing, and life was good, and the part about Mongo not being able to afford golf was very curious.

The family had the beach below the ranch set up for a party with tables covered in bright Hawaiian patterns and two different fire pits with all kinds of great smelling stuff cooking over open flames, a large canopy covered the tables, and folks played guitars and ukuleles and sang, just exactly the way you would picture a Hawaiian luau in your mind.

Shortly after dark, the torches were burning bright, and a couple of healthy, young men came carrying a very dead and very cooked pig on a giant silver platter. We dined on roast pork, three-finger poi, smoked sweet potatoes, grilled pineapple, and an abundance of things I didn't recognize; Lucy made sure I tried everything and was gracious about it.

Do you know how hungry the first person would have had to have been to eat three-finger poi for the first time? I've seen what they go through to make it with all the pounding and mixing and pounding some more, all just to come up with something that tastes like wallpaper paste that has gone bad. What person was so hungry that he/she ate that without first being hammered?

The three of us sat in between Mongo and his parents and made small talk throughout the two-hour meal. Somewhere around 10pm, an hour or so past my normal bedtime, we began to say our *thank yous* and *goodbyes,* and we, ok I, staggered to the big Mercedes and headed back to our bungalow.

My phone rang as we pulled into the resort and found our parking place,

"This is Roc!"

"Mr. Roc, this is Mrs. Pau, Mongo's mother..." and then there was silence on the line. I could hear her crying in the background.

"Yes, Mrs. Pau...what is it, my dear?"

"It's Mongo, he's dead! He's been shot, and I would like to ask you to help us figure out who did it."

I told Lucy and JJ about the tragedy, and JJ went on to his room, and Lucy decided to go back to the Pau ranch with me.

"Papa, what do you suppose this is all about?"

"I'm not sure, but you know how I feel about coincidences, right?"

"Yeah, I do," and she got very quiet.

The Maui cops and the State Police had arrived just minutes ahead of us, and there was still a lot of confusion. Lucy and I started walking towards the main house, and we saw Mongo's parents walking in our direction.

We hugged, and Mongo's mother was a little more composed than on the phone.

"Mr. Roc, Mongo was very impressed with you; he had done his homework on his computer, and he was going to ask for your help tomorrow, and..." she began crying again,

"And now I'm asking."

Mongo's old father stood beside her with red, swollen eyes, unable to speak.

"Yes, ma'am, anything I can do, just let me know."

"Mr. Roc, find the person who killed my Mongo!"

"I'll do my best, Mama Pau."

I called her *mama* but in reality, she probably wasn't but a year or two older than I.

Russell Eepo was Mongo's second in command and turned out to be a very likeable, very capable cop, and after talking to Mongo's mother, he was more than willing to share any information he had with me.

"Call me, *Eepo*."

"Like the song from *Blue Hawaii:* 'Eepo eats like fish go out of style?'" I asked.

"You're very perceptive, Mr. Reese."

"Please, call me, Roc, and I'm a huge Elvis fan!"

Almost all of the adult Hawaiians were crazy about Elvis Presley as his songs, and his movies had done great things to boost the economy of the Islands in the early 60s, and nothing had changed almost 60 years later.

Mongo had been shot in the chest, long-range from a craft that no one saw, and the surf had covered the noise of the shot as it probably had been suppressed. From the looks of the wound, it came from a large-bore rifle. Whoever shot it, probably used night-vision goggles, and it definitely was not an accident or spur of the moment assassination. This was a planned killing, and I had no doubt it was connected with good ol' Charlie Morgan's death.

It was well after 2am by the time we got back to our shack on the beach, and we sat down on the lanai with a large Crown and let the weight of the day melt away.

"What's the plan, papa? Kinda seems like it's gonna get stickier before this is over."

"Yeah, babe, I believe it very well may. I guess I should put JJ on a flight home in the morning as he won't be much help when the *ship hits the sand*."

The next morning, I awoke to my cell phone ringing, and I tried unsuccessfully to check the time as I answered it,

"This is Roc!" I said with what seemed to be a mouth full of gravel, or eggshells, or something.

"Baby, I just put JJ on a plane, and I'm heading back. I could sure use some eggs and some of that amazing juice."

"What time is it? Who is this, and what are you doing in my head? Get out, out, I say!"

"It's 10:15 and get yer lazy butt out of bed and meet me at the club house!"

I laid my head back down on my pillow for another 30 seconds, then I decided I didn't want to keep Lucy waiting, so I headed for a shower and a shave, donned lightweight linen slacks, a Tommy Bahama camp shirt, and driving moccasins, and I was out the door with a spritz of Palmaria aftershave. I couldn't wait to see what kind of an outfit Lucy had in store for me this fine day!

She was just extracting her beautiful self from the big Mercedes as I rounded the corner to the front of the clubhouse. She was a glorious sight with an amazing tan, navy blue, skin-tight, stretch shorts, and a red, stretch T-shirt with a sparkly American flag on the front that seemed to wave as she walked, and white patent, leather heels that made her calves pop as she moved towards me, and all I could do was smile.

"Hey, love!"

"Good morning! You look all bright and shiny, and I love that aftershave!"

"Thanks, girl, speaking of shiny, you look amazing as always!"

She smiled and kissed my cheek, and we walked into the dining room arm-in-arm.

"JJ's plane should be in the air just about now; he really didn't want to leave, but he wasn't ready to be shot at either."

"I understand; what I wouldn't give for a full weeks' vacation without someone trying to kill us, ya know? All I need is Crown, great food, and you and me on the golf course."

"Sounds perfect. What do we have to do to get a week like that?" she asked.

"I don't know; maybe find a deserted island with no phones, just you and me?"

"Sounds wonderful, but who would manage the golf course, do the cooking, and give us massages?"

"Why do you have to be so logical? I was just describing a perfect getaway."

"Well, let me know if you find such a place. I can be ready to go in three or four minutes."

"Let's finish this mess first, and then we'll try and find it."

We drank Kona coffee and ate large spinach and swiss-cheese omelets and breakfast meats and drank juice and sighed deeply, and life was bearable, at least for the moment.

Mama Pau was on the other end of my cell phone as I finished the last few drops of my coffee,

"Mr. Roc, good morning. I wanted to invite you to come stay at the ranch; we have a guest house that I know you will enjoy, and of course, the price is right..."

Lucy heard the conversation on speaker phone and shrugged her acceptance.

"Ok, give us a little time to check out and gather our belongings, and we'll be there as soon as we can."

"Thank you, Mr. Roc! Thank you so much! I'll be waiting," she said, and the phone went dead.

"What do you suppose that's about?"

"I'm not sure, but I know it's gonna save us five grand a night until we leave, but you know that doesn't include golf, right?" and Lucy smiled; she always seemed to get my humor.

Hole 5

I pulled the big Mercedes off the highway and onto the private road of the Pau Ranch, or farm, or pineapple orchard, or whatever the hell it was, and up to the main house. At the gate, a big, Hawaiian guy pointed towards a beautiful cottage on a bluff that overlooked the ocean. With all the excitement, I had completely overlooked it on our first two visits.

I drove up in front of what looked to be about an 1800-square foot, tropical island paradise. We went inside, and things just kept getting better. Everything was teak wood (the beautiful *Tectona Grandis* tree). The wall coverings, cabinets, and furniture were all made of the beautiful wood, and the wood looked old like it had come from the forests of Indonesia or Myanmar, not the equally beautiful new wood from the tree farms of Costa Rica and surrounding South American countries that are getting into the market.

There were large screen TVs in every corner of every room, a fully-stocked, gourmet kitchen with a large basket of fresh tropical fruit, including my new favorite the Mahuha Mowha or whatever, and a fully-stocked bar. I also saw a lava rock shower in the master bath big enough for all my best friends and a jacuzzi tub that was nearly big enough for Lucy to swim laps in. I looked for more bedrooms but there were only two. Both of them were masters, and both were amazing to see, made me want to call a halt to the rest of the day and take a nap!

I had just about convinced Lucy that some *afternoon delight* was the way to go when a knock on the door shook us both back to reality,

"Hey, Mama Pau, how are you doing, my dear?"

"Mr. Roc, we are going to bury my son this evening at sunset on the beach; you and Ms. Lucy will join us."

Her demeanor had completely changed from the last time we met; she was matter-of-fact and stern and seemed to have fire burning in her eyes and soul,

"Of course we will!" I said, and before I could say anymore, she turned and walked back the way she had come, stiff and straight as a board, almost like she was forcing herself to stand to keep from falling.

"What was that all about?" Lucy asked as she came out of the bedroom.

"Mama Pau invited us to the funeral or ordered us, I'm not exactly sure which; either way, she is not the same sweet lady we met a few short hours ago."

"Well, hun, the death of a loved one will do that to a person; not everyone can just push it aside like you do as though nothing happened."

"Whaddaya mean? Are you saying I have no heart?"

"No. I'm saying you handle death unlike anyone I've ever known; that's all."

"I'm sorry; when I lost my daughter and grandson, and then my wife, Jeanie, something inside of me changed. I feel really sick inside when I see a helpless animal mistreated like a dog or cat for instance, but when it comes to humans, not so much; most of them are truly stupid and deserve everything they get."

"Yeah, especially if you're the one who gives it to them, like a bullet between the eyes, for instance."

"Ok, this conversation is going nowhere in a hurry, and I can see I'm gonna end up the bad guy."

"Oh, Papa!" she came to me and kissed me on the top of my head. "How about a Crown?"

"I knew there was something I wanted beside you," and I winked, and then came another loud knock on the door,

"Good afternoon, Roc; can I call you, *Roc*?"

"Of course, Eepo! Come in; can I get you something to drink?"

"I'm fine; well...ya know...a bottle of water would be great."

"We haven't settled in quite yet; let me find one. Lucy, how about some ice water for Eepo?"

She came out of the kitchen with a large water tumbler filled with ice and three-quarters full of my favorite drink and a plastic bottle of water for our police friend.

"What's on your mind, Eepo? Any leads so far?"

"A couple of points of interest, but nothing concrete; have you come up with any reason for all this, Roc?"

"Only that both deaths are definitely related, and I hesitate to mention it, but Mama

Pau has had an attitude adjustment, and the change is not for the better."

"What do ya mean by that?" Eepo asked with some trepidation on his face.

"Well, when she was here a few minutes ago to tell us about the ceremony tonight, everything about her had changed: no more sweet, little ol' lady or granny-type, almost like a CFO of a giant corporation. She was all business with no sign of any grieving, just a strange transformation, you know?"

"Wow, that doesn't sound like Mrs. Pau. I'll definitely look into that! What else have you observed that I should be aware of?"

"Not much, so far, but we just arrived and haven't had time to look around or speak to any of the ranch hands; maybe by morning, things will come together a little more."

Eepo finished his water and left us alone in the guest house, wondering if he was being completely honest with us.

"What are your thoughts about the police officer?" Lucy asked as she walked about the beautiful interior of the guest house.

"You know, I could spend some serious time in this place, I think."

"Well, if we're still welcome here when this whole thing is over, we might just do that, and as far as Eepo is concerned, the jury is still out on him. I truly hope he's one of the good guys cause I don't know who else to go to with our findings."

We sat on the guest house lanai and finished our drinks; afterward, we dressed for the funeral. I hoped it was casual because we didn't bring any other clothes with us; just then, I heard a loud knock on the door, and upon opening, I saw a very large Hawaiian gent with an arm full of lovely, Hawaiian sportswear.

For me, there was a pair of expensive khaki shorts, a floral Hawaiian shirt unlike any I had ever seen, and an exquisite pair of flip-flops, and for Lucy, there was an amazing black Mou-Mou with embroidered Polynesian flowers in bright colors and a pair of flip-flops as well; she added some turquoise baubles to her outfit, and we were ready for a Hawaiian funeral. I really don't know how she does it, but the hits just keep on coming; she looks amazing in everything!

About 45 minutes before sunset, a large, gray-haired, Hawaiian gentleman showed up at our front door in a six-passenger golf cart and chauffeured us down to the beach, the same location as the other evening, but there were some visible differences: the family was dressed in very special ceremonial garb with lots of flower leis, and everyone was barefoot, although most were wearing sunglasses as we were staring into the setting sun.

Another difference was that instead of the many smaller fires going like the other night, there was only one large bonfire that roared 25 or 30 feet into the air, and there was a very crude raft made of logs tied together at the edge of the water. In the background, standing on a large boulder about 30 feet above us was a long-haired, almost naked, islander playing a conch shell and a beautiful, dark-skinned girl singing in perfect harmony.

About ten minutes later, the body of Mongo was brought down to the shore on the shoulders of four monstrous, beach boys; it was wrapped in white linen and placed on the raft, then covered with branches of local foliage. The four hefted the funeral craft out to waist-deep water, and another young man lit a torch from the bonfire and walked out into the surf, touched the brush that was obviously soaked in some kind of accelerant, and the funeral barge went up in flames. One of the beach boys pulled up the sail at the front of the craft, and the hot wind coming from the fire created a huge force that propelled the craft out to sea.

Mama and Papa Pau stood in silence for several minutes as the funeral pyre skipped through the small waves and got smaller in the distance, then mama Pau's emotions finally got the best of her, and she collapsed in the sand. Papa Pau tried with all his might to keep her from falling, but he didn't have the strength to hold her upright; several members of the family were at her side almost before she hit the ground and guided her softly down.

Her demeanor had changed again from a sweet, warm, welcoming Hawaiian princess, to a grieving mother, to a hardened business executive, to a woman out of control of her body and mind, sitting in the sand completely overwhelmed by the last few days.

Back at the guest house close to midnight, Lucy and I sat on the lanai, drank a cocktail, and listened to the surf crash on the shore and on the cliffs a little further up the coast. The full moon reflected off the water, and everything was absolutely beautiful; it was just too bad the situation wasn't different.

After a brief tumble in the comfortable, king-sized bed, I dozed off and didn't move until the morning light came through our bedroom window along with a fresh breeze off the Pacific Ocean; it was difficult to tell if it was a very cool morning and warming up, or if it was very warm and the breeze from the ocean was cooling it down. Ever been in that situation where you weren't exactly sure? It might be a *senior* thing because it seemed to be happening more and more.

Lucy brought me a steaming cup of Kona coffee, and she looked like she had just come out of the surf as she had a large bath sheet wrapped around her gorgeous frame and knowing her, there wasn't a wet swimsuit laying around anywhere.

"How was the water, my dear?"

"Amazing! I swam up the coast a ways and met a couple of curious sea lions, and when they got too close, a dolphin came up and escorted me back down the coast; the whole experience brought back memories of Port Aransas. You know, as beautiful as this is, I still prefer the Texas riviera for everyday living.

"Yeah, I think you're right. We could go broke very rapidly trying to maintain our lifestyle in a place like this. Why don't you get dressed, and we'll wander over and see how Mama Pau is doing this morning."

"Give me about 10 minutes, and I'll be with you."

Ten minutes? Have you ever known a woman who could walk out of the ocean and be ready to be on the go in 10 minutes? I looked at my watch at 7:43; I heard the shower come on, and exactly 9 minutes and 38 seconds later, Lucy stood in front of me wearing red shorty-shorts, a white, scooped-neck T-shirt with some sparkly things on the front and navy-blue heels; her hair was all curly from the shower, but I knew it would dry to an amazing full head of blonde gorgeousness.

"You are a total contradiction to the female race; do you do that to keep me confused?" I asked.

"Do what?"

"Never mind!"

We walked the quarter mile to the main house with the cool trade winds that were blowing off of the ocean into our faces, what an incredible morning!

"Good morning, Mr. Rockland! Mr. and Mrs. Pau are expecting you; please come in."

A very heavy, dark-skinned woman in traditional dress with a fresh flower lei around her neck lead us through the palatial Hawaiian home to the dining room.

We sat down at a hand-carved, teak table that would seat 20 or more. There were four place settings at one end that were set with juice glasses, three plates stacked one on top of the other, large coffee mugs, and water glasses filled with ice. There was a fruit bowl in the center of the table that held every kind of tropical delight imaginable, including my new favorite, *maca mucha* or whatever. Mr. and Mrs. Pau came to the table and were seated just seconds after us.

"I hope we didn't keep you waiting, ma'am. I didn't realize we were doing breakfast."

"Not to worry, Mr. Roc; we knew you'd be along, eventually, and by the way, Ms. Lucy makes a beautiful sight with the ocean as a backdrop at daybreak," Mama Pau said, and Papa Pau sat quietly as a large smile appeared on his brown, wrinkled face.

"Thank you," Lucy said with a slight grin, showing no other emotion.

We ate eggs cooked to order, fried, sweet potatoes, large slices of grilled ham and pineapple, and all the amazing assortments of island fruits and juices in silence, for the most part, until Mama Pau spoke up,

"Mr. Roc, how much do you know about the Pau family?"

"In what respect, ma'am?"

"Have you researched our family on the computer?"

"I'm not really a computer guy. I guess I fell through the cracks when it came to electronics; however, Lucy is the computer whiz for the company."

Before I could go on, Mama dropped me like a hot oyster shell and turned her attention to Lucy,

"So, Ms. Barnes..."

"Oh, please, call me, *Lucy* if you don't mind."

"Of course, Lucy, so what do you know about the Pau family?"

"Actually, not very much at this point; by the time we got settled in and after attending the funeral last evening, I really haven't had a moment to look at my computer; is there something you would like us to be aware of, ma'am?"

"Please, call me, *Mama*."

"Yes, ma'am."

I was sure Lucy was being condescending as she wasn't afraid of or overly disrespectful to anyone unless she had a good reason.

The Pau family is Hawaiian royalty; we can be traced back to the beginning of the Islands' first population from around 300AD, and the Polynesian people came by dugout canoes from the Marquesas Islands over 2000 miles away. What I'm saying, Lucy, is that our family has been a respected part of the Islands since the beginning of recorded time, and..."

Lucy interrupted her,

"Yes, Mama, is there anyone who you can think of who might not be as proud of your heritage as you are?"

"What do you mean, Ms. Barnes?"

"Lucy,"

"Yes, yes, I meant, *Lucy*."

Mama Pau was visibly shaken.

"Is there someone who thinks maybe you are not the right ones to have all the honors and privileges that go along with the royal family?"

"Lucy, there are over 400,000 Hawaiian people as close as we can tell, and I am sure not every one of them is happy with the royal family just as not everyone is happy with the president of our United States."

Lucy just shook her head in agreement.

"Has anyone made any threats on any of your family members, recently?"

"Just the normal crackpots trying to get under our skin, thinking they should have a better life even though they haven't earned it or worked for it."

"Do you have a list of the most recent threats? Obviously, one or more of those people were very serious about their feelings."

"I know Mongo kept track of the ones who sounded like more than just kids playing, and Eepo would have access to that list. Should I give him a call?"

"No, that's fine; we'll catch up with him after a while. We have a few calls to make back to the mainland, first."

We walked back to the guest house, and along the way I said,

"Nice job, girlfriend, looked like you almost got under her skin!"

"Sorry, I wasn't trying to. I was just trying to get some information."

"You don't have to apologize to me; if it had of been me asking the questions, we'd probably be headed to a hotel about now."

"Well, something is definitely not what it seems to be around here; do you see enough cattle or pineapple to live the lifestyle that we're seeing?"

"Not really; more like just enough to put up a good front, if you ask me. I don't know about the price of beef or pineapples on the Islands, but it would have to be pretty good to make it with such a small amount of land, and I haven't seen anyone working the fields or tending the stock...very strange. We need to search that computer thing of yours and see how much the royal family makes off of the Islands for being who they are."

"I think you're right."

Minutes later Lucy called me over to the desk,

"Hey, Roc, look at this!" Lucy looked up from her computer screen.

"What is it, babe?"

The Hawaiian people keep a residence for the royal family on one of the other islands, but they are not required to live there although if they don't, their annual subsistence stays with the property for maintenance."

"And just how much is this *subsistence*?"

"It looks to be around five-million bucks."

"Wow! I could *subside* quite well on five-mill; it would be a shame to have to give up those kinds of bananas."

"It doesn't appear that they have been giving it up; according to this article, the Pau family has found a loophole and have been collecting it for many years, or at least the last 20."

"That's 100-million, and it explains a lot about the ranch, plantation, and their lifestyle. I can see why some people may harbor some ill feelings toward the royal family."

"And also according to this, the Paus may have invested some of their inheritance into some pretty questionable enterprises like the kind that goes up your nose although there is no concrete evidence linking them to the drug trade, but there are lots of innuendos!"

"And it appears that the profits just keep going up, and I'd be willing to bet a bundle that this is not the information that Mama Pau wanted us to uncover; all we need to do now is make the connection between the richest man in the world, good ol' Charlie Morgan, Mongo, and the Pau family."

"Could it be that Charlie just liked the thrill of the race, saw the opportunity to make big profits with lots of customers running around the Islands snorting and partying, then heading home, no harm, no foul?"

"Yeah, girl, sounds like the perfect business: a captive audience with lots of cash in their pockets and the police captain to oversee and patrol it all."

"Yeah, but something must have gone terribly wrong to whack two high-profile folks like Mongo and Charlie."

"I think we need to shut this computer thing down and get out of here for a while; if Mama finds out where we're going with this, we'll be sitting targets here in this shack that I'd kill for back in ol' San Diego."

I drove the big Mercedes off the Pau property at a normal rate of speed, so as not to arouse any suspicions; it was going to be extremely hard not to draw any attention to ourselves on such a small piece of land. That's the problem with being landlocked: there is nowhere to run, nowhere to hide, and everyone knows your business.

The village of Lahaina, or at least it was a village the last time I was there in 1975 or 76, was where the Hawaiian people held the Whaling Festival, celebrating the catch and the bounties from the sea even though whaling had been banished many years before to protect the dwindling number of whales. Lahaina was now a bustling city, hosting somewhere around two-million tourists a year.

We found a parking spot about a block and a half from the police station and made our way through the crowds of shoppers and eaters, and everyone without exception turned to take in Lucy's beauty as we walked by.

Russell Eepo did not seem surprised to see us. An aid brought us steaming, giant mugs of coffee, then he closed the office door as he left the room.

"So, Roc, what's up at the plantation? How are the Paus treating you?"

"They are the perfect hosts under the circumstances, not really sure if there is anything we could learn about the murders out there, though; what have you come up with, chief?"

Eepo took a couple of extra seconds to look at both of us before he answered like maybe he was trying to see into our souls to see what we already knew.

"What do you know about the Pau family?" he asked.

"Not much, except of course, that they are royalty and quite wealthy."

"That's an understatement! They may be the richest family between the Orient and the States!"

"Wow!" I said with a modicum of surprise added to my voice. "How did that happen?"

"Well, there's a lot of speculation about drugs and smuggling, but Mongo went out of his way to keep a lid on any of the stories. I have found out more in the last two days than I have in the last 10 years now that I have access to his private files."

"So, what do you suppose Charles Morgan had to do with any of this? My thought is that he was just a player, in it for the action, like a game of golf, and ended up in the wrong place at the right time."

"We're not a 100 percent positive at this time, but that sounds like a very good assessment of the situation," and Eepo looked into Lucy's beautiful blue eyes and lost his train of thought for three or four seconds.

"Do you have any ideas about any of this, Lucy?"

She looked at me, and I gave her the go ahead. As near as I could tell, good ol' Eepo was one of us, and we could trust him. She began to expound on her findings from the Internet a few hours earlier.

As Lucy was talking, my mind began to wander back to a golf course in the San Diego area a few months after I returned from my stay in the "Valley of the Sun."

JJ had set up a match with a couple of middle-aged businessmen, maybe late 30s or early 40s, you know, real old guys, or at least they seemed old to us at the time. However, the moment I met them in person, I realized they were probably criminals of some sort. They were a little too crude and not really dressed for golf with the exception of the shoes. They seemed more like guys at a rodeo who wanted to be seen as cowboys because they bought boots and hats but didn't have the worn out jeans and work shirts to go with the look; you know, you can just tell.

We played for several hundred dollars more than we could afford, so as not to offend them, but we also couldn't lose because we didn't have the money to pay them; it was one of those dilemmas where we could die either way. After about three holes and being two down, I took JJ aside for a strategy session, and we decided we would rather be dead with a pocket full of cash than *dead broke* if you get my drift.

We stepped up our game and ended up winning about $1800 each and decided there wouldn't be a rematch as they were just too scary. Although we hadn't done anything wrong except maybe win, it was hard to figure what was going on in their minds. So, we bought our opponents several cocktails, which may have not been a good idea, then headed for our favorite steak and seafood house for a quiet dinner.

About halfway through the shrimp cocktail and our second beer, tires squealed, shots rang out, pitchers of beer exploded, and people (including JJ and myself) dove for the floor. The outside patio at Jaxon's was normally a very quiet place to watch the sun go down, and it was there that we first had our introduction to a young police officer named Dan Brown (later to become Chief Brown SDPD).

He came over to the two of us and said,

"I have looked all around, and you two are the only things out of place here, so ya want to tell me what's going on?"

I looked at JJ, and he looked back at me, and we tried to discern if what we had done on the golf course that day was illegal. I took the lead as JJ was kind of shy when it came to altercations,

"Well, Sheriff..."

"I'm not a sheriff. I'm a police officer!"

So much for my attempt at humor to calm the situation, and I explained our exploits on the course that day to Officer Dan as well as their outcome.

"How about some names?" he asked.

"Larry and Moe...I think."

"And where was Curly on this fine day?"

"Really, Sheriff, I mean Officer, those are the names they gave us, and far be it from us to argue about someone's name."

"Okay, okay, so you got into a golf match with two of the three stooges and rolled them for $1800 and pissed them off, is that right?"

"That sounds about right, Sher... ah, I mean, Officer, and we'd really like you to catch them before one of those slugs taps one or both of us!"

"I'll see what I can do; don't leave town, and I'll be in touch."

About two days later, JJ and I were at the local driving range hitting practice balls and eating lunch at an outside table when JJ saw our two opponents/enemies walking toward us with their worn out bags over their Hawaiian shirt-clad shoulders and pork-pie hats and looking just as goofy as they had a few days earlier.

"Ah, Roc, we got company."

"Who is it?" I asked with a smile on my face, thinking it might be the pretty waitress or some beach girl who had taken a liking to me.

"The San Diego mafia."

I knew exactly who he meant, so I slipped my hand into the side pocket of my golf bag and pulled out my Colt .38 Police Special with a one-and-a-half-inch barrel that I kept close by ever since I got out of the Coast Guard; it just seemed like the thing to do given the profession that JJ and I had chosen to pursue.

A mere second or two later, I saw JJ diving for the deck, and I followed suit, pulling my golf bag over the top of me for whatever protection I could gain as bullets started bouncing off the tables and chairs and other customers. When the two emptied their pieces, I took close aim and put three rounds in each of the SOBs and left them soaking up the California sun face-down on the deck.

Obviously, the police had been called, and our new friend, Officer Dan, came right over to us upon his arrival,

"Reese, are you going to be a thorn in my butt?"

"Whatever do you mean, Sheriff?"

"I mean, there are dead people everywhere, and you have a smoking gun; that's what I mean!"

"Well, Sheriff..."

"Don't call me that! I'm not a sheriff!"

"Yes, sir, sheriff, just think of how many more might be dead if I didn't have this *smoking gun*!"

"Ok, so let me see your carry permit just to keep it legal while we sort this thing out, and which ones are the bad guys as if I didn't know?"

"That would be them in the Hawaiian shirts and goofy hats Sherrr...I mean, Boss...ah...Officer, and I'm not sure about where I put my permit. I may have misplaced it."

"Do you have any idea who these guys are?" he asked.

"I didn't until a few minutes ago, but I do now: they are really bad golfers dressed in clown suits, and now they're dead."

"Not exactly the information I was looking for, but I guess you nailed it. As soon as you get released from the crime scene, you head straight for the station, and I'll get you a temporary permit to carry until you can find yours," and he winked at me, and I breathed a sigh of relief.

That was the beginning of one great friendship that's been going on for almost 40 years.

I snapped back to reality as Lucy was just finishing up her recitation on the royal family, and Eepo was shaking his head in agreement.

"Yeah, Lucy, it sounds like you've got a rather good handle on them for the moment. I'm checking into Charlie's background to try and find a paper trail, but he could easily have hid his involvement in a 100 separate places or more likely, all the transactions were made in cash. He may have a cargo container full of currency buried in his backyard, for all I know."

"Well, Eepo," I broke in, "I think we have done just about all the damage we can do around here, so we're gonna be on our way; call me if you come up with anything new," and we left his office.

"How about a drive around the Island, maybe hit some balls and grab some lunch along the way?"

"Sounds like a great idea to me, hun," and Lucy flashed one of her five-million dollar smiles my way, and I just melted.

I had forgotten that the maximum speed limit on Maui was 35 mph if I ever knew it. There wasn't that much for a couple of golfers to see when we got outside of town, only volcanic rock, sand, and desert landscape, so when we finally made it to Kipahulu, we called it a day. Luckily, we found a quality hotel that had just received a cancellation, and I managed to talk the sweet girl behind the desk into letting us have the room for a mere $500 with free happy hour and breakfast. I guess it could have been worse.

While we were sitting at the bar that evening indulging in Crown Royal Reserve on ice and waiting for our table to become available, I got those little prickly sensations that I get from time to time when certain people want to do serious harm to my body, and I grabbed Lucy's hand and whispered,

"Put your hand on your gun and be ready."

"What is it, papa?"

"Not sure, but I have a hunch that something is wrong, and you know my hunches."

"I do," and she removed her hand from mine and pushed it down into the small clutch bag at her side.

I swiveled my barstool slowly, so as to not attract any attention, and when my right side was to the bar, I reached under my camp shirt and pulled my out Glock 19, silently chambered a .9mm round, and let the pistol hang at my side.

I saw in the mirror behind the bar, men entering the room, and I motioned for Lucy to look, so we were on the same page. There were three very large Hawaiian or maybe Polynesian gentlemen (why do people start calling folks *gentlemen* when things turn to crap? Why not three assholes with guns?) who entered the bar, and we were stuck up against the bar with no place to run.

"When I give you the word, get behind the bar as fast as possible!"

"Got it!"

As soon as the lead bad guy focused on us and started for his piece, I said,

"Now!" and we both leapt over the bar.

I motioned for Lucy to head to the far end, and I headed in the opposite direction; fortunately, there were only a couple of patrons in the bar besides us, and I pushed the bartender to the floor as I came over and ordered him to stay down.

How in the hell did they know where we are, and what do they want? We must be onto something, I thought to myself.

Bullets began to fall like raindrops, and they were more than just your everyday semi-automatic handguns. Liquor bottles and expensive glassware shattered and crashed to the floor all around us; it wouldn't take much to set off a good fire with all the alcohol pooling around on the floor. No sooner was that thought gone from my mind, then a spark from a round hit behind the bar, and flames billowed up to the ceiling.

I saw Lucy laying prone at the end of the bar, and I did the same at my end.

I was thinking, *Ok, Roc, make every shot count!*

I was limited to 15 rounds and Lucy to 10. I wasn't sure what this was about, but it was clear they didn't want to talk, so I took dead aim at the guy on the left, knowing Lucy had the guy on the right.

No survivors, Lucy-girl, and I squeezed the first round off, hitting my guy between the eyes. Then, I put two more in his chest, and I saw Lucy's guy take one or two in the heart area, and we both let loose on the middle bandit and filled him with at least eight or nine rounds between the two of us, and then the room got deathly quiet.

"Everyone stay down!" I yelled, but the shots and the fire had the few bar patrons spooked, and they were up and running around, screaming.

The bartender emerged from behind the burning bar with his clothes on fire, and I grabbed him, threw him to the ground, pulled an imitation leather covering from the nearest table, and smothered the flames from his clothes; luckily, nothing was harmed, just some minor burns, and although he was in shock, he managed to mouth a "Thank you!"

The maintenance folks came bursting through the door and had the fire under control before it could take over the room, and I could hear sirens blaring in the background, both police and fire trucks. I managed to find a brand-spanking new bottle of Crown Reserve still in one piece, and I cracked the seal, handed the bottle to Lucy, and waited for my turn; that pretty much took care of the top half of the bottle.

I thought,

If we can find a couple of glasses and some ice without broken glass in it, I can pretty much guarantee what's going to happen to the bottom half of this bottle.

Acting Chief Russell Eepo was the third cop through the door,

"Eepo, what the hell are you doing here? If you're following us, you need to stay a little closer!"

"No, Roc, I was on my way to visit my sister when I heard the shots; she lives just down the road a mile or so."

"Does this mean we'll be able to get some dinner and a good night's rest?"

"Don't worry, I know the manager of this joint. I'm fairly sure I can get you fed and comped!"

"Ok, not too bad for the busy season; would you happen to have an ol' pair of Wranglers, a T-shirt, and maybe a bikini for Lucy to slip into, or maybe we'll just squeeze the booze out of our clothes into a glass, drink it, and call it a night."

Just about that time, a very large and jovial Hawaiian gentleman who I assumed was the manager came up and shook my hand,

"Mr. Reese, I'm David Pau, the manager of this hotel. If you folks want to go to your room and start freshening up, I'll have everything you need sent up, and you can dine on your lanai," and he handed me a key.

"I have my key with me," I replied.

"Not like this one."

"Any relation to Mama and Papa Pau of the Lahaina Paus?" I asked.

Oh, Rockland, what a stupid question! Use your head! I said to myself.

He just smiled.

He handed me a gold fob with a microchip, "What number?" I asked.

Just use this in the elevator, and all will be revealed.

I wasn't sure where this was going, but I guessed we'd see soon enough.

Lucy and I dragged our beaten and alcohol-soaked bodies into the elevator, and a voice came over the small speaker on the wall,

"Please scan your key," and a blinking, red light showed from a small, quarter-sized hole on a brass panel.

I passed the fob in front of the lighted panel, and it turned green, then a voice came back,

"Thank you, Mr. Reese."

I looked at Lucy, and she looked back and just shrugged.

Ok, I have stayed in a couple of presidential suites in my time (not necessarily invited), and all I can say is this must be the king of the world's suite!

"Mr. Reese, Ms. Barnes, if I could ask you to go and shower, your masseuses will be here directly," a concierge-type guy greeted us as we entered the massive suite.

He didn't have to ask twice.

I washed her; she washed me; we washed each other, oh, Lordy, we were so clean!

After our massages, it was time for dinner.

They (someone) had our dining table on the patio set for a king with platters of chilled crab, shrimp, and lobster, fresh-shucked oysters and clams, and those were just the appetizers. Also on the table was the freshest Caesar salad with the most amazing dressing I had ever tasted with bread that tasted like it had just been baked outside our door. We spent over an hour working our way through the first couple of courses that included a seafood and cheese bisque that tasted like we were sitting in the ocean beside the pot as they prepared it.

Now as you may recall, I'm not real big on wine, but we had one of those wine servers with the keys to the basement, and he told us to just leave our wine pairing to him. He ordered for us a selection of whites, pinks, and reds, and afterward, a fine cognac, and I finally had to wave them off, throw up, or explode! Besides, it was way past my bedtime.

Somewhere in the wee hours of the night (I didn't remember) the crew had cleaned our room, and when we awoke, it was spotless.

I noticed a large pot of coffee and pastries of every kind on a large silver tray sitting on the dining table. I thought, *Are you people friggin crazy? We just finished eating dinner!*

However, the coffee was the best I had ever tasted, bar none!

There was a handwritten note that read:

Mr. Reese & Ms. Barnes,
I can't express enough our gratitude for the amazing courage you displayed and the countless lives of hotel employees and guests whom you saved.
You are welcome as our guests at this establishment from now until the end of time. Please don't stay away too long.
Very truly,
Your friend, David Pau.

"Hey, babe, come take a look at this!" and she stepped to the door from the sleeping quarters with a bathrobe open all the way.

"Hey, papa, come take a look at this!"

I got to my feet to take a much closer look, and the next time I looked at the clock, it was 10:47. We dressed in some of the finest clothes I had ever put on my back, compliments of our new friend, David Pau.

It was 11:30am when Eepo came a calling,

"Hey, Roc, those outlaws were permanent employees of the King and Queen of Hawaii."

"Are you saying they worked for Mama Pau?"

"That's what I'm saying!"

"What in the hell could be their reason for wanting us dead?" I asked.

"I'm thinking you dug a little deeper than they expected."

"But how could she possibly know that?"

"If I were a betting man, I'd say the guest house was bugged just like your car, which explains the three thugs in the hotel bar last night, and I took the liberty of removing the bug from your vehicle."

"Well, CRAP!"

"Uh, oh!" Lucy said out loud, and Eepo looked in her direction,

"That's not good. I wouldn't want to be in the Pau's flip-flops from here on out."

"Roc, can I ask you not to do anything stupid, unless I'm with you?" Eepo asked with a smile.

"As long as you don't fall too far behind, I can live with that, but I don't take kindly to someone trying to put holes in my lovely girl, here."

"I thoroughly understand; maybe you should spend another night or two here until we can put a plan into action."

"Oh, no!" Lucy chimed in, "That would be terrible! I don't know how I could possibly bear it," and she faked some misery.

"I think I'm going to slip into a swimsuit."

"Lucy, you don't have a swimsuit."

"I know," and Eepo's slanted eyes opened wide,

"Oh...my...can I stay and watch?"

"I think your work is done, here, Chief," she said as she left the room.

The private pool in our suite was not large, but just how much water did Lucy really need to get that lovely body wet and without a suit to absorb any excess amount? I'd say the size was a perfect fit, and so we turned on the bubbles and popped the cork on a bottle of the house's best bubbly and let the world go by.

Ok, Mama P...bring it!

By seven o'clock we had received word that the restaurant and bar were ready to reopen and that our private table would be available at whatever time we decided to come down.

It was nine-thirty when we walked into the private dining room, and the special service where it left off the night before began all over again. I could really get used to being treated like this, or maybe we already had? This was paradise, no doubt about it!

Hole 6

The next morning, my cell phone rang, and I checked the clock on the nightstand: 7:10, not exactly the time I would have chosen to wake up, but all in all, I felt pretty good. The other side of the bed was empty, and I could hear the shower running.

"This is Roc, what's up?"

"Roc, Eepo, here."

"Yeah, Chief, what did ya find out?"

"More than I really wanted to know, I'm afraid."

"What's it all about?" I asked although I was pretty sure anything Eepo had to say wouldn't come as much of a surprise.

"It looks as though your friend, Charlie, was funneling large sums of cash to the Islands by purchasing land that the Paus didn't have the right to sell, and he was building large warehouses on said property and titling them to Mama Pau."

"So, I guess they were in cahoots?" I asked already knowing the answer.

"It looks like they were partners in the import/export business and probably warehousing drugs for others who were doing the same."

"And maybe Mama Pau decided she needed a bigger piece of the pie, maybe enough to even kill her own son?" I asked as a cold streak ran down my back, giving me the chills. Damn! Some people really piss me off!

"Or at the very least, Mongo was collateral damage," Eepo replied, and then a cool change came over him as though a strange entity had crawled up inside of him and curled up for a nap. I could feel it through the phone.

"I have to go," he said, and the line went dead.

"What just happened?" Lucy asked.

"You look white as those 8000-thread count sheets you're lying on."

"I'm not real sure, but I think we need to get back to Lahaina. Let me get dressed, and I'll go check us out and meet you downstairs."

"No problem, papa. I'll be right behind you."

David Pau was in his office as I was heading for the front desk, and I knew he saw me, but he did not acknowledge my presence. *Hmmm...*that feeling came over me again, *What in the hell was going on?*

The very lovely *wahine* at the desk presented me with a leather folder with our initials embossed across the bottom and all the receipts had been stamped "PAID IN FULL."

I thanked her and turned to walk away, and David was standing behind me, a change of heart, maybe?

"Mr. Reese..." and he reached out to shake my hand.

I grabbed his, but it felt like a dead fish, the complete opposite from the bubbly, appreciative man of two days earlier. Had a family member gotten to him?

He said a brief and insincere *Aloha*, and he was gone, headed back to his office.

I met Lucy at the elevator, and we headed to the car that was waiting with the engine running just outside the automatic doors.

"I'd say they're in a hurry to get rid of us; it's scary how quickly things can change. I guess gratitude for saving one's life just doesn't go as far as it used to."

"Roc, what's going on?"

"I'm not exactly sure, but we're not nearly as welcome here as we were yesterday. Are you sure you bathed this morning?" and she put a well-placed elbow in my ribs that almost took my breath away.

"Not even funny, Rockland!"

The drive back to the tourist trap of Lahaina was long and uneventful even though the company could not have been any better, and Lucy looked like she just had jumped off the cover of a fashion magazine.

Have you ever noticed how slow 35 mph is when you're really in a hurry to get somewhere? I kicked it up to 70 and kept one eye on the road and the other on the rearview mirror for *Johnny law*. Lucy's eyes kept going from me to the speedometer and back again, but she didn't say a word. I guess she could sense the necessity that was not open for discussion.

"Would you turn the radio on to Channel 19, please? That's my favorite Sirius channel."

She did, and Elvis was on; he was halfway through "Blue Hawaii," how apropos!

The big Mercedes tore up the highway, and the miles flew by.

We walked into Eepo's office at 4:15, and Lucy looked at him and then at me. There had definitely been a change in the man.

"Roc, would you please close the door?"

I did, and we took a chair and waited for him to say something,

"I have been getting emails and texts since early this morning from untraceable sources with threats on my life if I don't drop this investigation, and I do believe they're serious."

"Well, based on the events of the last week or so, I'm inclined to agree with you, snuffing out a police lieutenant and a couple of tourists should not even make the needle on the *murder meter* wiggle; the fish are too little, I would imagine. I don't know what your plans are from here on out, but I suggest you have a couple of your most trusted men beside you at all times."

"I was thinking of staying close to you two."

"Well, sheriff, we would definitely enjoy the company, but it would increase the size of the target on our backs by about 33-percent but suit yourself! If we're going to do this, we need to dump our Mercedes and check out an

SUV with some armor; would that be a problem?"

"No, I already have one being brought around along with a skilled driver who used to be special forces and has been back from the Middle East for just over two years."

"That should work just fine, then."

We walked down the steps of the police station and standing beside a 15-passenger SUV was a guy who looked like Dwayne "The Rock" Johnson on steroids, clad in one of those stretch T-shirts, wearing jeans with a 28-inch waist. He had an assault belt with a .45 caliber Colt in a canvas holster strapped to his thigh with five or six extra magazines in separate pouches, two pairs of handcuffs, and several, heavy, plastic, riot restraints stuffed through his belt. I didn't see a survival knife, but I was sure he had at least one folding weapon on his person, more like two or three, and probably another pistol strapped to his calf.

Eepo made the quick introductions,

"Randall Jones, this is Lucy Barnes," and he nodded to acknowledge her presence.

I reached out my hand, big mistake! HOLY CRAP! I could feel bones starting to break and tears welling up when he shook it,

"It's great to meet...you?"

"ROC!" I said with phlegm in my throat, making it almost impossible to be understood, and he let go just in time for me to keep from screaming out loud, "WTF!! Jesus! I'm so glad you're on our side!"

Eepo mentioned, "Normally he dresses a little better, but a couple of altercations destroyed both pairs of his slacks and sportscoats, and as you can guess, they need to be custom-made to fit."

"He looks fine to me!" Lucy piped up.

"Yeah, I certainly wouldn't tell him he was underdressed," and everyone smiled, even Randall.

We headed north in the big SUV with Eepo riding shotgun and Lucy and I in the back.

"Where we headed?" I asked even though I was sure I knew.

"We need to go to the Pau's ranch and get your belongings. I'm pretty sure you won't be welcome there any longer. I'll put you up at my place; it won't be quite what you're used to, but the price is right, and you can fall out of bed into the ocean if you're so inclined."

"Sounds charming," Lucy said with a smile.

"Just don't get your hopes up too high, and you won't be too disappointed."

A short ten minute ride later, and we passed the Resort and then came to the entrance to the Pau's plantation. Everything was quiet, which gave me the feeling that it might be deserted.

We gathered our clothes and doo-dads and loaded them in the back of the SUV while our man, Randy, stood guard.

"Looks like the Paus were expecting company and weren't in the mood to visit."

"It certainly looks that way. We'll take a short ride to my place and let you get a feel for the *poorer side of town* while we ponder our next move. I have an idea we're going to be doing some island hopping."

Eepo's place was about four miles farther up the coast, and as it turned out, it backed up to the Pau's property although there were no buildings or structures for the last two miles or so.

The land between the highway and the Pacific Ocean was very overgrown, and the vegetation began to take on the look of native Hawaii.

When we pulled off of the highway, my mind immediately took me back to the early Tarzan movies that I loved as a kid, and the Saturday matinees with 15 free color cartoons, tall coco palms, banana trees, and all the native flora and fauna you can expect when you visit the Islands.

Lucy was bouncing around the back seat, looking in all directions,

"I don't care what the house looks like, just give me a cot, and I'll sleep out here; this is gorgeous!"

A couple more blind turns, and we came out of the jungle and onto the beach, and OH MY GOD, the view was amazing! Eepo's place was a wooden cottage on stilts, which was about four feet off the ground with a huge front porch that had a half a dozen chairs looking out over the beautiful Pacific. It looked to be about 1800 square-feet, and it was perfect for a bachelor, at least. The furnishings and decor were traditional Hawaiian or Polynesian, and I could see Lucy's designer eye getting the best of her.

Eepo showed us to what looked like the master bedroom, and we declined it, not wanting to put him out of his room, so he showed us the private part of his house that opened up onto the beach as well. There were two bedrooms and a great room with sliding doors that allowed the complete front of the house to get the trade winds when they were open.

"Eepo, this spot is absolutely beautiful! How did you ever find it?" Lucy was inquiring and decorating at the same time.

"It's been in the family since the early 1700s, and each one of us who takes it over does improvements to make it our own. I have lived here on my own since my parents died in a car crash about three years ago. I actually grew up here, then I went into the military and lived in town when I got out, but this is home, now."

"I envy the girl who ends up living in this paradise; is there no one you want to share it with, Eepo?"

"There is one lady; you'll meet her tonight at dinner."

Randy had our bags unloaded and in our room and was ready to head back to town.

"It was good to meet you. I am familiar with your adventures, and I'd like to talk with you before you leave the islands."

"Absolutely, *Rock*!" I said with a smile.
"Any time!"

"Don't call me, *Rock*!" he said. Then he smiled a very large smile and winked as he walked towards Eepo.

"We should be fine, but I'll call you if we need you, and we'll see you for sure at about 10 in the morning," Eepo waved him off, and Randy drove away.

Eepo turned to us and said,

"There are swimsuits in the closet; that's about all we wear around here, and I'm about ready for a swim and a cocktail, not necessarily in that order; how about you two?"

"Absolutely!" I replied, and Lucy shook her head in agreement.

"What's your pleasure?"

"Well, normally, it's Crown on the rocks, but I'm sure we're open for whatever you have."

Eepo opened the wooden doors that hid a humongous hand-carved bar, and his stock was incredible.

"I have been told I make the best Mai-Tai on the islands, but you're welcome to whatever you prefer."

"I'd love a Mai-Tai," Lucy said as she headed for the bedroom to change.

She came out sporting what could only be called the "perfect bikini," cut from the most gorgeous Hawaiian cloth I had ever seen!

"No sense spoiling the party; count me in!"
I said, enthusiastically.

Now for you *tee-totalers,* a Mai-Tai is a
traditional rum drink that is made with white
and dark rum, and Eepo added a splash of
medium rum just to make it his own. It also
contains fresh lime juice, Orange Curacao, and
orgeat syrup with a splash of fresh pineapple
juice. Mix everything together except the dark
rum, pour over ice, then float the dark rum
over the top, garnish with a piece of fresh
pineapple and a slice of lime and look out!

First of all, the glass was big enough to
hold four Crown on the rocks, and B, there was
enough alcohol to put the average social
drinker under the table; fortunately, Lucy and I
were way above the social-drinker level, or so
we thought.

The last time I had a Mai-Tai was 1973
while I was stationed at the Coast Guard base
just off Honolulu at Sand Island. I had met this
young, attractive, teacher from Oklahoma, and
we decided to have a drink or two at the bar at
her hotel before I showed her the nightlife of
Waikiki, and she showed me what there was to
do at night in Oklahoma.

Have you ever been kicked in the head by a
mule because that's just about the feeling I had

the next morning from drinking too many Mai-Tais.

I woke up naked on the beach with people all around and no cute, young teacher to ask what happened. I was arrested for lewd behavior, indecent exposure, and for vagrancy and a couple of other things I don't recall. What I'm trying to say is that a Mai-Tai will knock you down in the dirt, walk away, and leave you there, so be careful!

Lucy took a sip, and her eyes lit up, and a big smile came across her face,

"WOW! That's the best thing I've ever put in my mouth!"

I looked at her with a look of disappointment.

"Ok...the second best thing."

I took a large sip, and all those old memories started flooding back into my head; the inside of my jowls began to tingle, and my stomach began to retch, and all of a sudden, there I was once again, sitting at the bar with that sweet, young teacher from Oklahoma, and she was force-feeding me Mai-Tais, and I was letting her, thinking we were going to be together forever or at least until morning, whichever came first. It was all starting to come back: I vomited in her lap just before I fell backwards off the bar stool, and then I ran out of the hotel, shedding my clothes as I went. I ran past the International Market place as Don Ho sang "Pearly Shells," and I think I saw Hilo Hattie wave as I went by. I think I just figured out why I never saw her again, not Hilo Hattie, but the teacher.

I spit and gagged and walked back out of the bathroom and ordered a Crown on the rocks, and Eepo smiled.

As we were about to sit down for dinner, I looked around,

"What happened to your gal-pal?" I asked.

"She got tied up at work, might be along a little later."

Lucy was on her second Mai-Tai, and I was expecting the worst, but she was holding her own. A little, old lady served us dinner, and we ate fresh fish with mango, jalapeno, and pineapple relish, baked, sweet potatoes with garlic butter sauce, and an avocado and roasted tomato salad with Hawaiian sweet bread. Did you ever notice how much better food tastes by the ocean?

Mai-Tais definitely made miss Lucy amorous, so we took a moonlight swim and drank another cocktail, and I had one of the best night's sleep I've had in many years.

In the morning, I awoke to the sun reflecting off of the water and a cool breeze coming through the open doors, and I truly believed I could lay in that bed from then on. There was just something about mornings on an island paradise that was like no other: the air smelled fresher, the water looked bluer, the fruit tasted more amazing, almost as though it had sparkling bubbles in it, that may be a little over simplification (sounds like a toilet bowl cleaner, but you know what I mean, but some things are just difficult for me to describe).

Lucy emerged from the water looking like Halle Berry in that James Bond film minus the bikini, and my neck strained to see every stride of her long legs through the sand. Wow, what did I do to deserve her, or what did she do to have to put up with me? Semantics, right?

We showered together in an outside natural waterfall that flowed out of a lava-stone wall just behind the beach house, and we were completely rejuvenated; we dressed, and our little, old, Hawaiian lady had steaming mugs of Kona coffee waiting as we came to the dining room table.

I was preparing to ask about Eepo when I heard a big SUV come around the last turn, and Randy and the chief stepped out.

"You guys are up and at it early this morning," I said as they came through the door.

"Some new information has come to light; are you two ready to go for a chopper ride?"

"Sure...where are we headed?" I asked.

"It looks like the Paus are on the run and going underground..."

In the middle of his sentence, things got deathly still, and I saw Randy look toward the SUV and then holler,

"IN-COMING!" and everyone dove for the floor. Four of us dove under the large, wooden table, and I felt the little, Hawaiian lady look up over my butt...ok five, and then the big government SUV lifted off the ground and exploded as it turned circles in the air and landed on its top, completely engulfed in flames.

Randy was up on his feet running towards the outside of the beach house; we all followed and gathered just below the deck, looking out to sea. He pointed at a speck moving away from us at a very rapid pace,

"Looks like a 14-or 15-foot Zodiac! Probably the kind the special forces use. I'd guess a 40-horsepower outboard, so they'll be out of sight in a few seconds; looks like two people aboard."

"Son, you've got some eyes on ya," I said as I squinted to try and see the speck way out on the horizon.

"Lots of special training, and they were firing an SSM at us."

"What's an SSM?" I asked.

I was too shook up to figure it out for myself.

"Surface-to-surface missile fired from a handheld device."

"Sounds like someone has access to some pretty sophisticated weaponry, and they're really pissed at us!"

Randy broke in, "I'm pretty sure it was just a warning cause they could have just as easily targeted the house and leveled it."

"Looks like we're on foot," I said to no one in particular, and Eepo spoke up,

"Not exactly! I'll be right back," and he took off running towards the jungle.

A few seconds later, we heard a powerful engine fire up, and tires squeal, then a white, custom Humvee came crashing through the banana trees and slid to a stop in front of us.

Eepo jumped out and signaled for Randy to take the wheel; we all climbed aboard, and tires squealed once more, and we raced by the burning wreckage of the big SUV that was lying upside down in the sand.

At normal speed, the police helipad would have been about 20 minutes away, but with

Randy's skills and at 85 or 90 mph, we covered the 17 miles in less than 10 minutes.

Eepo's Hummer was first-class: it had thick, saddle-colored leather throughout with an incredible Bose sound system, and who knows what else was hidden under the hood as it ran like it may have been supercharged, and Randy put it through its paces.

We pulled into the Hawaiian State Police helipad, and I immediately spotted what I hoped would be our ride: a jet chopper painted metallic orange and black with gold and silver pen-striping and a large decal on the door that was crested in gold and black with the initials *HSP* on it.

"Wow...that looks fast!" I said out loud.

"Yeah, it is the only one of its kind on the Islands," Eepo said.

Lucy asked, "And you are qualified to operate that machine?"

"No, I'm not, but Randy is, so let's get loaded up and on our way."

Lanai was only eight miles away, and at 180 miles an hour, or whatever, the monster helicopter flew, and we were there two minutes before we took off; I mean, it was fast!

A really big mistake that amateurs sometime make is swinging the golf club like a baseball bat and looking over the center field fence for that home run; most over-swing and lose control of the clubhead, and the perfect, opposite example of this is Jordan Spieth when he's really on his game; his backswing is about three-quarters of what the rest of the pros are, yet he hits it plenty far and with great accuracy. I knew the first time I saw him play, about four years ago, that he was bound for greatness. The only reason I bring this up at this time is because I hate to fly, and the monster bird in which we were zooming through the air at the speed of light was making me very nervous, and I was trying to distract myself.

Eepo must have noticed the look on my face, and he smiled at me and spoke into his mouthpiece, "Don't worry, Roc, Randy can fly anything with wings."

"That's wonderful and very comforting, but this thing doesn't have any wings," I replied as we dove towards the blue water, and I saw the grin on Randy's face.

"There it is! Hold on!" I heard Randy say as he forced the bird into an even steeper dive toward the water; all Lucy and I could see was the back of Eepo's and Randy's heads as we shot toward the Pacific Ocean.

"OH, CRAP! Randy cried out,

"MISSILE!" and he put the chopper into a right-hand, 360-degree flip, or twirl, or curl, or whatever the hell his flight instructor would call it!

I was upside down, looking under and through my armpit when I saw the smoke stream flash by our port, or was it our starboard side? Hell, I was upside down, and I didn't have a clue!

When we finished the roll and were upright once again, I looked between the shoulders of the two in the front seats, and the water was coming up at us so fast, I knew we were toast, soggy toast.

The Zodiac beneath us was getting bigger by the second, and just when I had a very brief visit with my maker and was "kissing my ass goodbye," Randy banked hard right, and the missile sailed by once again, and I heard an explosion over my left shoulder.

Lucy and I craned our necks to see the Zodiac flip high into the air and explode, and body parts and rubber boat pieces flew in all directions. Randy powered up, and we shot through the heavy, humid air and off toward a landing area on Lanai's south Hulopoe Bay.

Eepo's voice came over our headphones, "Well, so much for making a surprise entrance!"

Lucy spoke up, "Yeah...I'm pretty sure they know we're here unless the rocket went off by accident."

"You have an amazing grasp of the obvious, my love," and I received that all too familiar right elbow in my ribs.

"Damn, girl...I'm getting way too old for you to keep beating the hell out of me the way you do!"

"Sorry, love...it slipped," and that gorgeous grin came across her face as we flew through the sky at breakneck speed.

Hole 7

Lanai Island has a population of 3000-plus, and for the most part, the islanders are of Polynesian descent. The Pau family kept a residence there (if you can call a 6500 square-foot home on the beach a residence).

Eepo pointed the mansion out as Randy buzzed the very secure compound. Besides the large main house, there were also several outbuildings with two or three that could be considered guest houses and at least that many that looked like large storage sheds, and I noticed lots of folks with automatic weapons wandering about.

"Eepo, what the hell is going on? All this has to be about more than just a few pounds of dope; this seems more like old people willing to kill their own and stand against the Federal

Government for something I don't understand!"

"Yeah, Roc...this goes a lot deeper than drugs, and it's beginning to look like some sort of conspiracy against the free-world, maybe even the entire world!"

"Hey, today is Christmas Day, isn't it?" I asked as Lucy leaned toward me and whispered in my ear,

"Merry Christmas, darling!"

"Yeah, Roc, it is," Eepo answered.

"I think I left your present under the tree."

"Not a problem, my friend; just get me on the ground in one piece, and that will be plenty for me!"

"Not to worry, Roc! Randy's got that covered," and we headed for the hard deck coming in hot, and my stomach was almost in my mouth.

Randy put the bird down like a seagull with sore feet, and I sat still in my seat, waiting for all my body parts to catch up and settle back into their assigned places.

I've had *sea legs, and air legs, and no legs at all*; ok, not exactly the way George Jones sang it, but you get my drift. Did I mention that I am not a huge fan of flying, especially while sober, and I was definitely sober!

There were only three people at the air center/police station: the flight coordinator and two police officers, so Eepo rounded up the two cops, and the six of us jumped into a newer model, shiny, black SUV with official decals in muted silver all over it and headed into the jungle with Randy at the wheel.

"What's the plan, Eepo?" I finally had to ask as I was having a tough time putting the whole thing together to understand just how it was going to play out.

"Hell, I don't know! I thought we'd just drive in there and start shooting!"

"Ok, sounds like my kind of party!"

Randy smiled, and Lucy just shook her lovely head.

We drove about eight or nine minutes, then Randy turned on the bubble gum machine, thinking the flashing red and blue lights would hopefully, be enough to keep us from being blown to bits by automatic rifle fire as we entered the estate.

Now, I'll admit that I'm pretty comfortable flying by the seat of my pants most of the time, but that operation just seemed to have too many loose ends. Who were we going to fight and why? I just wasn't sure.

Randy threaded his way through the heavy growth that threatened to cover the road in some spots and through a very secure-looking, steel gate that open into the compound and stopped about 10 yards short of the massive porch that covered the entire width of the mansion. Two very large Polynesian-looking gentlemen had automatic weapons strapped across their chests with their fingers resting close to the triggers, and they were looking hard in our direction.

"Stay here and don't do anything to get me killed," Eepo said as he stepped out of the SUV and onto the white, sandy parking lot.

We watched as he stood between the two guards and spoke in a casual manner, not seeming to be concerned for his own safety.

About 40 or so, seconds later, he reached out and shook hands with the big Polynesian-looking guys and turned and came back to join us.

"They're not here," he said.

"Are you sure?" I asked.

"Yeah! I went to school with those two and as bad as they are, they're not going to lie to me; they may not tell me the whole truth, but that's another matter. Randy, you want to get us to the house?"

"Sure, Boss," and he dropped the shifter thingy into "R," and we squealed rubber backwards for about 30 feet, throwing sand in every direction. Then he spun the steering wheel, and the front end did a "180," and we were off in the opposite direction.

Now, I had yet to see Randy in any kind of combat situation, but if his ability to drive and fly was any indication of his qualifications, I knew I'd be feeling pretty comfortable right about then. I looked over at Lucy, and she was as calm as a fresh-picked papaya; she never failed to amaze me.

My mind flashed back to a time that JJ and I were on the practice tee at Torrey Pines, just minding our own business, enjoying the beautiful coastal day when this big Italian-looking guy with a crooked nose and muscles ready to burst through the arms of his not-so-expensive polo/golf shirt walked up and stood between us so that neither one of us could swing a club and didn't say a word. JJ looked at me, and I looked back at him and shrugged.

"Yes...can we help you with something?" I asked.

"Are you guys named *Reese* and *Johnson?*"

"Good guess," and I reached down and picked up a practice ball and handed it to him, and he looked confused.

"Oh, ya want to hold the ball down around your knees. I'm gonna try and cut it into that

100-yard flag," and I took a stance and wiggled my sand wedge just a little.

He looked at me, and then a light went on, and he dropped the ball and stepped back behind us.

"You're a crazy son of a bitch!"

"Whaddya mean? Why else would you be standing there if you didn't want to assist us?"

"The *man* wants to talk to you."

"What *man* would that be?" I asked.

"My boss."

"Does yer boss have a name?"

"Of course!"

"Well...what is it?"

"It's Albert."

"Albert, what, and who the hell is he, and what does he want with us?" I was starting to get tired of our stupid game.

"He has a proposition for you."

"Well, tell him if it doesn't have anything to do with golf, we're not interested; there's a bench right there, and we're in the middle of our practice session, so if he wants to talk to us, he's welcomed to come sit."

The big *wop-looking* guy's veins in his neck and biceps began to bulge, and we could tell he was getting perturbed.

"I can't go back and tell him that! Are you crazy?"

"Well, then, just sit down until we're finished, and I'll tell him myself, should be another 35 or 40 minutes."

"You are crazy! Do you know who the hell he is?"

"I don't have a clue!"

JJ and I were just about 30 or so and really hadn't had much involvement with the criminal types since we settled into a life of gambling on our ability to make a golf ball do what we wanted.

Anyway, it turned out that Arnold or Albert had some connections down in Mexico who loved to play high-dollar golf, and he saw an opportunity to make some fast cash without any risk of going to jail. Well, we talked and finally settled on a couple of thousand, our expenses and half the winnings. To make the story short, we ended up with about 20-grand each in our pockets, and good ol' Albert ended up in a ditch just south of the border about two weeks later. I guess I don't need to tell you that JJ and I kept a look over our shoulders for the next couple of months.

Randy got us back to headquarters in record time almost before Eepo had time to formulate a new plan of action.

"Where are we spending the night?" Lucy inquired.

"We have a safe house not far from the precinct; it's fully staffed, and we should be comfortable there."

Mama and Papa Pau were deeply concerned that they had completely underestimated Roc Reese and his friends. They had lost five of their most trusted bodyguards with no damage to Roc's and Lucy's investigation.

"We need to find a way to put a stop to this nonsense before they discover the entire operation!" Mama said to her spouse.

"Yeah, if they haven't already; they're putting an awful lot of pressure on us for folks who don't know what we're into. I believe we need to step up the pressure and get rid of them once and for all."

The couple sat in overstuffed leather chairs and nursed Mai-Tais in their secret location on the tiny island.

The safe house was more like a vacation home on the Gulf Coast and was a two-story complex that appeared to be about 3000 square-feet, built up on stilts with parking underneath, right on the water, and there was a golf cart parked in the driveway.

We took our things up to the second floor to one of the four bedrooms and made ourselves at home. Our room had a sliding-glass door that opened onto a small patio with two lounge chairs and a table, and it all looked out over the beautiful Pacific. I sat down in one of the chairs and fatigue rushed over my 60-year-old body.

"Lucy asked, "Can I get you a cocktail, love?"

"Absolutely!" and I laid my head back to relax and suddenly, I was standing on the tee box at Quail Run Country Club east of San Diego.

JJ and I had a match with a couple of judges from the area, and when I first met them, I began to really feel bad that we took that game as the poor, old guys were both in their 70s, and it was all they could do to hit the ball.

They both teed off on every hole with a five-wood, and I wasn't even sure if they could lift a driver. We gave them more strokes than we ever gave away in the history of the world, and it still wasn't enough to make it a fair match.

Hole Number 7 was a par 3 about 130 yards from the *old geezer* tees; we allowed them to play all the way up front while we played from the tips with 40 to 80 yards difference on every hole. Anyway, JJ and I both hit the green, and one of the judges rolled his five-wood to within about six feet of the green. The other teed it up, waggled 10 or 12 times, then swung his club with all his might. He was looking at the pin before the club ever got to the ball, and his ball squirted straight right, bounded across the cart path, landed about four feet off the Number 9 Green, then followed the contours of the putting surface and ran for what had to be 65 or 70 feet. Then it rolled up to the hole, hit the pin, bounced straight up in the air and landed on the front edge of the cup; it sat there for three, maybe four, seconds while we all watched, then it rolled in.

The old judge was ecstatic, jumping up and down, fist-pumping and all. I really hated to tell him we weren't playing that hole. He had never had a hole in one, so we went along with him.

JJ and I walked away with a grand each, had a great day, and made a couple of valuable friends in the process.

"Here ya go, love!"

My eyes snapped open, and the alluring miss Barnes was standing in front of me with a large glass filled with ice and about half-full of my favorite adult beverage, and she looked amazing as well.

"Thank you, babe. I guess I dozed off. What's going on downstairs?" I asked.

"Eepo and Randy would like to meet with you at your convenience."

"Well, I guess I better get my lazy butt downstairs and see what's on their minds."

Eepo and Randy were seated at the dining room table when I walked in,

"What's up, guys?"

"Come sit down, Roc; it looks like we have a handle on the Pau family. They have a hideout on the other side of the island, and according to my informant, they are well-fortified."

"So, do you think they are expecting us?" I asked.

"It certainly looks that way," Eepo replied.

"So, what's the plan?"

"Well, I think we'll start with a pile of fried fish and a few cocktails and regroup in the morning."

"I really like that plan, my friend!" I said, and I took a large pull on my Crown, and I could feel my muscles starting to relax.

Randy asked from his overstuffed chair,

"Hey, Roc...Eepo says you are a pretty good stick (means you're a good golfer); what's your handicap?"

"Well...yeah...I do alright, and I don't have a handicap."

He kind of gave me an inquisitive look, and I guess it didn't dawn on him that I might be scratch or a zero handicap.

"How do you play matches all over the country without a handicap?" he asked.

"Well, Randy, I haven't carried a handicap since I was 16. I'm a scratch golfer, and Lucy is a very solid four."

"Wow! he said, "You guys must make a great team! You beat their brains out, and Lucy makes them enjoy every minute of it!"

"That's pretty much the way it works, but we've never taken advantage of anyone. If anything, we give them more strokes than they ask for."

Lucy came down the stairs looking like a million bucks or more, and we enjoyed happy hour while we waited for the caterers to bring dinner, which turned out to be another great surprise.

They served us some kind of smoked, white fish wrapped in banana leaves, boiled shrimp covered with a pineapple and sweet-chili sauce glaze, roasted pork with a chutney sauce of some kind with lots of ginger and steamed rice, and the amount of food looked like it would be enough for ten people, but the four of us devoured it all and sat waiting for dessert.

Finally, two lovely Hawaiian girls came through the kitchen door with dinner plates with a dish of flan in the middle and covered with the most amazing brandy and caramel sauce, and a snifter of brandy was served on the side. By the time we finished eating, it was 9:30, and my eyelids were starting to get very heavy.

"If you boys don't mind, I'm gonna fill my glass and call it a night," I said as I backed away from the dining room table.

"Not at all, Roc; it's been a long day," Eepo replied.

Randy nodded goodnight, and Lucy said,

"I'm right behind you, love. Are you going to take me upstairs and ravish me?"

"I can take you upstairs, or I can ravish you, but at my age and condition, I can't do both; you'll have to decide which," I said without looking back.

Everyone smiled.

By the time I finished my half-full glass of Crown, I felt like a noodle, literally, maybe *al dente*, but a noodle, nevertheless.

"How about a little sugar, sugar?" Lucy asked as she laid beside me in all her magnificence.

"Absolutely! Help yerself," I said, not worrying about the obvious slur in my speech.

"Just take what you want and don't worry, I'll send you a bill in the morning."

The next thing I knew, it was 6:30 in the morning, and I was looking for a Coke or mouthwash or anything with bubbles to get the terrible taste out of my mouth.

"You must have been exhausted! I heard Lucy say from the bathroom, "I got coffee!"

"Oh, thank God!"

"Just sit tight, love. I'll bring it right out!"

And there she came wearing a towel wrapped around her blonde hair, and nothing else! Ah, hell!

The next time I looked, it was a quarter to nine, and I felt much better. I hit the shower, dressed, and headed downstairs to greet the day.

Randy and Eepo came out of their respective doors into the communal area. I was sitting in an overstuffed leather chair with a steaming cup of joe with my eye on *FOX News* when they walked up.

"Whatcha watchin, Roc?" Eepo asked.

"Well, since neither one of you saw fit to show up for my colonoscopy, I thought you might want to see the video."

"Oh, Lord, please, no!" Randy shouted.

"Not before breakfast, at least!" and that pretty much set the tone for the day.

"So, what have you come up with, Eepo? Are we just gonna walk in the front door and say *howdy* and start blasting away?"

"That may not be the best idea since they're well-fortified, but I do have a few more folks on the way to help out, so we can just sit tight and enjoy the Hawaiian hospitality until everyone is in place!"

Hole 8

It was close to noon when the gray SUV with four Hawaiian state cops inside pulled into the parking area of the safe house.

Sargent Paul Mukka and his deputies were dressed in khakis and navy-blue polo shirts with flak jackets and navy-blue ball caps with *HSP* embroidered in gold on the crown. Three of the four weighed in at 300 or more pounds, and Sargent Mukka was a smooth-running 250 if a single pound, they definitely were a whole truck-load of Hawaiian humanity.

We suited up and climbed aboard our respective vehicles and headed off in search of the fray. Randy was at the wheel of our shiny SUV, and Paul Mukka and his boys followed behind, trying to keep up with Randy's obvious superior driving skills. The island wasn't that far from one end to the other but trying not to raise suspicion meant driving slow and not too close together, so our 10 or 12-minute trip actually took about 20 or close to it.

Eepo had the Pau compound location pulled up on his tablet, and he was giving instructions over his mouthpiece to the other crew behind us. Lucy and I could hear the plan through our earbuds as well.

"We'll wait for you in the parking lot of Spanky's Burgers."

"No problem, Boss; we can't be more than three or four minutes behind you."

"Roger that! We'll see you there!"

It looked like the road was clear for a ways, and Randy put the hammer down; the super charger kicked in, and we all were pushed back in our bucket seats until Randy backed off the gas. We had to be doing close to a 100, and we all took a deep breath when the pressure left our chests, and the big SUV coasted for the rest of the distance to the parking lot of Spanky's Hawaiian Hamburgers,

Like No Others!

"Eepo, what makes Spanky's so special?" I asked.

"Well, first, they're made with fresh island pork, and second, they have pineapple slices on them with a secret, special sauce, so much so, that the recipe is protected."

"Protected? It's a hamburger, and they only have what... half a dozen locations?"

"Three, actually."

"And, they're worried about someone stealing their sauce recipe? Don't they have anything more important than that to worry about?"

"Hey, some people's moral compasses just lead them astray even in Hawaii," Eepo said.

"Yeah, a moral compass can only point you in the *right* direction. It can't make you go there," I replied, and everyone laughed.

We sat at the back of the parking lot behind Spanky's, and exactly four minutes later, Paul Mukka and his crew pulled into the space beside us.

"Suppose we should feed the boys before we take them into battle?" I asked, "Wouldn't want them to try and fight on an empty stomach."

Eepo smiled, "You may be right. Hey, you boys want a pig burger before we head off to war?" and the doors of Paul's SUV flew open, and a ton of manhood raced towards Spanky's.

"Maybe we should hang back here until the dust clears," I said.

Now, I've had some pretty damn good burgers in my 60 years, but I have to say the Spanky's special was absolutely terrific! It was made with two quarter-pound patties, flame-broiled to perfection, two large slices of goat cheese, the freshest lettuce and tomatoes I believe I've ever had, and a special sauce that I guess people would die for, and oh yeah, two slices of fresh pineapple. The whole burger felt like it weighed three pounds, and it was impossible to get your mouth around.

I looked over, and Lucy had finished hers.

"Lady, are you nuts?"

She wiped her lovely mouth and swallowed then said,

"Oh, papa, that was amazing! The absolute best burger, ever! We need to look into getting one of these back home!"

After the burger joint, we had just settled down in our respective vehicles ready to proceed when Paul's SUV exploded into flames and left the ground. It did a backflip and landed on the passenger's side, and the explosion, glass, and flaming metal flew in all directions with pieces bouncing off of our ride.

Randy dropped the big SUV into low-gear and floored the foot pedal, and we shot out of the parking lot and into the street, burning rubber as we went.

"What the hell is going on around here?" I yelled at Eepo as another explosion rocked the fire-ridden vehicle carrying Paul and his crew.

"DAMN IT! Eepo exclaimed out loud.

"Mama and Papa Pau have pushed me far enough! I'm gonna take them down, and I don't give a damn if they are the *Royal* family! Where the hell did that missile come from, Randy?"

"From the air as close as I can tell," he replied.

"Well, then, find us some cover, so we can regroup."

We traveled a few miles at breakneck speed, while Eepo talked over the radio to headquarters, requesting backup and EMS, knowing full-well that all the occupants of the big SUV were toast.

Randy hit the brakes, and we slid sideways, then he accelerated, and the tires caught, and we were off down a dirt road for about a quarter mile then began to slide again. We came to a stop under a large grove of trees out of sight from any overhead assailants. We all took a long hard breath then exhaled.

"Damn the Paus!! Those were some good men, and all of them were friends of mine," Randy lamented.

Thirty minutes later, Eepo had finished his correspondence with headquarters, and we were formulating our own plan to put an end to the Pau Dynasty once and for all.

We had a satellite view of the Pau property that sent pictures each time it circled the Earth on Eepo's tablet, and it looked like the only way into the complex was right up the middle through the front gate or from the Ocean, and we didn't have any boats handy.

"Oh, well, let's do this dance!" I said, and everyone nodded their heads in agreement.

It looked to me like there were only two guards in the front, and I asked Eepo,

"Are they friends of yours?"

"I hope not, because this time, we're going in with full fire! Ok, Randy, let's get this over with! Hit it!" and Randy put the pedal to the metal, and the big SUV roared, and sand and gravel shot out from all four tires, and we lurched forward.

The iron gate was no match for the bull-bars on the front of the SUV, and we hit it at 30mph and didn't even slow down. Both sides of the solid structure flew off the hinges and onto the manicured grounds.

Randy put the big rig into a power slide as we worked our way around the fountain in the middle of the brick driveway just as bullets started flying in our direction.

Eepo and I had our AR-15s out the window on the passenger side, and when the first rounds hit our truck, we opened up on the front of the house about 50 yards away. I emptied a full magazine and slammed home a second and began to fire again while Eepo reloaded.

I saw one shooter take a knee, then go face-down, and the second one bounced backwards off the wall of the house, then he went down to his knees with one arm in the air, and it was over.

Randy slid to a stop in front of a massive porch that had a covered parking area, and we all piled out with our guns at the ready. The front door of the house was unlocked, and we followed Randy in, single-file, with one of us peeling off each time we came to a room.

Lucy went into what looked like a home office on the left, and I heard her holler,

"CLEAR!"

Eepo took the first room on the right, which was a bedroom,

"CLEAR!"

Randy took the kitchen, and I went left into what looked to be a very large family room. I heard Randy yell,

"CLEAR!"

I saw the back of a head just above the top of a leather armchair, and I yelled,

"Raise your hands above your head, NOW!" but got no response.

"Raise yer hands!" I repeated my order at the top of my voice as I inched closer.

Mama Pau had never looked lovelier, albeit the bullet hole in the side of her head did make a slight mess of the makeup on her right cheek.

I let my rifle sag to my chest and called out,

"Clear, but I got a body!"

Lucy came in with her Glock at the ready and stood beside me,

"Whaddya suppose this is all about?" she asked.

"Well, doll, I'd say that Papa Pau finally got fed up with Mama's bullshit!"

Randy and Eepo finished clearing the rest of the house and came in to look at Mama Pau,

"Whaddaya think, Roc? Looks like a small caliber .22, maybe, .32 at the largest?"

Just one shot to the soft spot in the skull of an aging person was about all that was needed. The side of her head where the bullet entered was slightly enlarged and distorted, but other than that, Mama Pau looked fairly normal and pretty content; her eyes were a little glazed over, but all in all, the ol' gal didn't look too bad.

"It doesn't look like she was expecting it by the expression on her face, pretty normal. I'd say Papa surprised her. I guess we need to rethink who's in charge of this operation after all."

Eepo asked, "What in the hell are we looking for? Randy, any ideas?"

"Well, Boss, neither air nor sea, there just aren't that many places to hide on this island. It's way too small! He's got to be here, somewhere."

"Right! Randy, get on the horn and lock down the airport, no one in or out until further notice! Roc, will you and Lucy give the rest of the property a good going over, while I get the Coast Guard involved? We'll meet back here when we're finished."

"You got it, Eepo!" and Lucy and I took off to see what we could find.

One of the outbuildings we came across looked more like a resort with living quarters that any bachelor would die for. It was very well-kept and had a big-screen TV, leather furniture, stainless-steel appliances in the kitchen, and a single bedroom decorated to the *nines* by whomever had lived there.

We stepped out the door that opened into the warehouse, and all at once, the hair on the back of my neck began to stand up. I raised my hand to keep Lucy from walking ahead of me, and she stopped and raised her gun. I looked in all directions and saw pallets with four, red 50-gallon, plastic, drum-like containers stacked two high, two rows deep, and each row was about 10 pallets long. I didn't know what was in them, but I assumed it was a lot of drugs.

We moved cautiously into the warehouse, and I saw movement from the corner of my right eye, and then I heard something that sounded like a teenager's voice,

"Please, don't shoot...don't shoot me!" and a very skinny, young lad stepped out from behind the last row of pallets with his hands held high above his head,

"Please, don't shoot! Ok?"

"Don't worry, son; we don't want to hurt you. Walk up here!" I ordered.

"Who are you?" I asked.

"My name is Rulie, and I keep the warehouse clean and put the labels on the drums when they come in. I also drive the forklift and load and unload the trucks."

"How old are you, Rulie?" I asked.

"I'm 15, sir."

"Do you go to school?"

"Ah, no, sir; I just work here."

"Where are your parents?"

"They were killed in an accident a year or so ago, and the Paus took me in and gave me this beautiful place to live in."

"Do you have any idea what's in these barrels, Rulie?"

"No, sir. Mr. Pau said the contents are very dangerous and to never open any of them!"

The 50-gallon drums were beginning to get the best of my curiosity,

"Lucy, baby, will you go see if you can find an office or someplace where they keep the paperwork? I want to take a look in one of these drums and see just what we're dealing with here."

"You got it, babe!" and she walked off towards the back of the warehouse.

"Rulie sit down over there and relax while I decide what we're gonna do with you."

"Yes, sir, but you're not gonna shoot, are you?"

"Not if you don't make me, kiddo. Just relax, ok?"

"Yes, sir." and Rulie took a seat on three stacked pallets in the corner and cupped his head in his hand.

Lucy yelled out, "Hey, Roc, you need to see this!" and I headed towards the back of the warehouse.

Lucy was in a small office just large enough for a desk, a chair, a small filing cabinet, and a wall safe that was standing open and was mostly empty except for a half a dozen stacks of U.S. $100 bills, probably the remnants of what wouldn't fit in a *go bag*.

There was some white powder on the top of the desk, and Lucy was just taking her finger out of her mouth as I walked in.

"This is the real McCoy, papa!"

"How would you know that?" I asked.

"Just because I'm blonde doesn't mean I'm stupid; it's the real thing, very pure *H*. If all those containers are full of this stuff, we're talking billions of dollars' worth of dope!"

Randy rounded the corner and whistled,

"Wow...that's a pretty good chunk of change to leave lying around!"

Eepo came in just seconds behind him and said,

"I popped the lid on one of those drums out there, and it's filled with gallon baggies of what looks to be pure *H*. If it is, this could be the biggest drug bust in the history of the world!"

On the other side of the island, Papa Pau and a half-dozen of his closest confidants were huddled around a dining room table in a small cottage on a private ranch.

"Listen up, it's time to leave this place! It has been our home for many years, but things have changed, and we need to move on; anyone who does not wish to make the journey is welcome to stay behind. Check with Mr. Makaha here, and you can draw your final pay."

One man raised his hand, and the other five knew that it was the very last mistake he would ever make.

"My dear wife will not be coming with us this trip; she has fallen ill and requires medical attention. He smiled to himself, (*Just a bit late for that!* he thought). Gather your belongings, and we'll meet at the heli pad in 15 minutes," and the six men headed off in all directions to prepare for their journey.

Papa Pau and four of his men were seated in the eight-passenger helicopter, and the roar of the engine completely masked the gun shot from the small cottage. Then Mr. Makaha walked out the door towards the chopper with his overnight bag in hand.

Randy yelled at Eepo to get his attention as we inspected more of the plastic drums, each one stuffed to capacity with gallon freezer bags full of pure heroin.

"Boss, I just got word that a chopper has crossed into open water headed out to sea without a flight plan and is not responding to hailing."

"Can you find out where it originated from?"

"Workin on it!"

Two minutes later...

"Eepo, it took off from the Wiihulu Ranch on the northside of the island about 14 minutes ago."

"What do we know about that ranch?" Eepo asked.

Our tech guy is running down as much info as he can find, but it looks like the Paus may end up being the landowners there as well."

The ATF showed up to take over the inventory as we were leaving, and Randy put the big SUV through its paces, while Lucy and I hung on for dear life and rattled around in the back seat.

"I called ahead; the chopper is fueled and ready to go!" Eepo's voice was loud and clear in our earbuds.

With sirens and flashing lights on high, Randy maneuvered down the small country road and then onto the highway and into town without incident, but he definitely put the fear of God into a few old men and women who were out for a leisurely drive, passing some on the right without them even knowing we were around, then cutting back to the left and across the double-yellow line, then sliding back to our lane and flooring the big motor once more.

We power-slid to a stop about 10 yards from the idling bird, and we all piled out and ran for our seats.

"Everyone strapped in?" Randy asked, and we all responded in the affirmative.

We were in the air in a matter of seconds, hurling skyward like a bullet. We reached maximum speed, and I reached for Lucy's hand and squeezed it gently then closed my eyes, and my mind drifted back to calmer time when JJ and I were sitting in our golf cart waiting for the group ahead of us to clear the tee and nursing our tumblers of Crown Royal Reserve.

We were playing a couple of high-powered businessmen from Dallas, Texas, and they were very good, but just not good enough to beat us.

Dale made a smooth and powerful swing, and the ball soared until it caught the very last tree down the right side of the fairway and kicked dead right, then came to rest just behind a boulder about the size of a Volkswagen Bug, unplayable.

"Jesus Christ, the people who gave us golf and called it a game are the same friggin idiots who gave us bagpipes and called it music!" he said with a very humorous, Texas drawl.

His playing partner teed up, waggled several times, took a deep breath and exhaled, looked left, then at the ball, and took a mighty swing. His extra-large belly swayed with the motion of his swing, which pulled him off balance just enough to allow him to hit the ground about three inches behind the ball.

His driver bounced over the ball, nicking it just enough to roll it off the tee about eight or nine yards at which point, he attempted to break the very expensive, very strong graphite shaft over his knee; unfortunately for him, the shaft was much stronger than he was, and when it reached maximum velocity, it slipped through his sweaty hand and snapped back to its normal shape. The only problem was that his head was in the way, *WHOP!* The grip of his club made perfect contact with the left side of his face, starting at his jaw line and ending at his temple. He looked stunned for several seconds, then tears came into his eyes.

I looked at JJ with a slight smile on my face,

"Yer terrible!" he said, trying not to break out laughing.

Just then, the wounded Texan threw his club with great vigor, and it ricocheted off of the ball washer and straight back into the forehead of his playing partner who was standing just off to his left.

Dale went face-down like a toe sack full of onions hitting the deck.

JJ very calmly said,

"The follow through is the part of the swing that takes place *after* the ball has been hit but *before* the club has been thrown!" and we both broke out laughing.

JJ and I each put $1600 in our pockets, and our opponents went directly to the emergency room after paying their dues. We only played 15 holes that day, and it just seemed like a perfect day to spend at the bar watching the bikini-clad girls make their way back and forth from the pool area.

I snapped back to reality as the big chopper in Randy's very capable hands slashed through the clouds in hot pursuit.

I really dislike flying, and it seemed like I hadn't had a drink in days. Then the thought came into my mind that when you get older, falling seems just like flying for a little while, except at the very end. I squeezed Lucy's hand, and she smiled back. She was having the time of her young life.

"Hey, Eepo, what's our plan for after we land?"

"Well, Roc, I thought we'd just swoop down and kick the crap out of the bad guys and then go have a Mai-Tai or two."

"Sounds like a winner to me!" I said with all sincerity.

Hole 9

Papa Pau was settling into his luxury cabin, one of several that had been created onboard for very special stowaways of means.

His four bodyguards were housed in another cabin, less fancy, but suitable enough with plenty of prepared food and beer in the fridge and lots of booze to make the long trip bearable, and it didn't take them long to partake of the bounty.

We had just cleared the coast when a large chopper passed us on the port side, coming from the Ocean, and Randy said,

"If I were a betting man, I'd say that's the taxi that the Pau party was on."

Eepo looked closely, then hailed headquarters on his phone,

"Yeah, HQ...there's a large bird heading your way. I recommend you have a party waiting for it when it lands and then get back to me with as much info as possible."

"Will do, Lieutenant," and the line went dead.

Randy spoke up, "As close as I can tell, they're about 45 minutes to an hour ahead of us sooo...that would make the ship they're on about 25 miles or so, out to sea. Whaddaya think, Boss?"

"We can't kick their asses until we find them, Randy!"

"Yes, sir!" and I could feel the big bird increase in speed as we all sat back in our seats.

It seemed like we flew for hours before Randy came over our headsets,

"Looks like we got a target up ahead, Boss!"

I looked between the high-backed, bucket seats of the chopper and out through the windscreen and couldn't see a thing but the ugly, green Pacific Ocean, and the hair on my arms and neck began to stand up,

"Ah, Randy...ya might want to take it a little slower...." then ALL HELL BROKE LOOSE, and we were upside down and falling, then bouncing off the water and rolling, and then everything went black!

I opened my eyes and discovered I was face-down in the rolling sea that had five- to six- foot waves lapping all around us. I forced myself to turn over onto my back although the pain in my side and back was excruciating.

I saw Lucy bobbing up and down and started to swim in her direction. When you're in severe pain, traveling even a short 10 yards can be exhausting, but I pushed on.

I grabbed the collar of her life jacket and pulled her close to me,

"Are you ok, ol' girl?"

She moaned then answered with a very weak response,

"Did you get that SOB who hit us, papa?"

"Not yet, kiddo, but this thing's not over yet!"

I heard some very loud moans like a wounded elephant or rhino, and the left side of the chopper broke water and floated about 30 or 40 feet from us, and I started swimming in that direction with Lucy in tow.

Randy came around the front of the bird and raised his hand for us to stop. He unhooked himself from his life jacket and entered the chopper through the door just behind the pilot's seat and disappeared.

A few seconds later, we heard a giant belch, and the bird went face-down and headed for the abyss.

Oh, crap! That's not good!

I had a nagging, helpless feeling in the pit of my stomach, not only because of the loss of a friend, but for being lost and alone in the middle of the Pacific Ocean without a single person aware of where we were.

"What now, papa?" Lucy asked through shriveled lips.

"Looks like we swim, kiddo; you wouldn't happen to know which way is north, would ya?"

The sun was almost down, and the sky was turning an eerie shade of purple, and it looked like we were in for a hell of a storm. *Just f--g perfect* was all I could think of.

It seemed like hours since the chopper had headed for the bottom, apparently I was wrong because of a sudden, a bubble started breaching the surface, then more and more, and then a bright, orange, rubber raft broke the surface and shot 10 or 12 feet into the air with Randy trailing behind, holding onto a mooring line.

He cleared the water with such force that good ol' Randy flew right over the top of the raft, and we heard him yell "YEEEHAAA" as he flew through the air, and he landed in open water on the far side.

"ARE YOU, OK?" I shouted.

"HOLY CRAP WHAT A RIDE!!" he screamed. "Are you two, all right?"

"Yeah, we're good, but I could use some dry skivvies if you've got a pair handy."

"Sorry, no, but if you can find a line hanging down that side of the raft and toss it over here, we'll see if we can't get this thing upright."

I told Lucy to stay close, and I made my way to the side of what looked to be a 16- maybe, 18-foot inflatable life raft. I found the line and heaved it over to Randy.

"I could use yer help, if you guys can make it around to this side."

We made our way around to the far side of the raft where Randy was treading water.

"Where's yer vest?" I asked.

"I don't know, but there are more on the raft; help me pull this thing over, so we can get out of the drink."

We gave it one big tug and nothing.

"Lucy, are you up to lending us a hand?" Randy asked.

"Yeah, I think so,"

Another big tug, and still nothing.

"Life rafts aren't designed to be on their backs, kinda like turtles," he announced to no one in particular.

"Let me get underneath and see what I can come up with."

"Hey...Randy...you need to hurry; yer bleedin pretty good from the side of yer head!" I said.

He wiped his head with a wet hand and then said,

"Yeppers; if there are any sharks within a couple hundred miles, they're probably on their way," and he disappeared under the rubber craft.

A faint voice from under the raft came across our ears,

"On three, pull with all yer might! One...two..." and a giant *swoosh* of air came, and the raft lifted about four feet out of the water.

"THREE!"

Lucy and I put our backs into it, kinda hard to do from a floating position, but nevertheless, it worked, and the black bottom flipped over, exposing the bright OSHA-orange, top side of the raft that now had a roof over it.

Randy popped up at the bow and hollered,

"Get aboard before we all become food for the fishes!"

We were just about to settle in when we heard another voice from out in the water a ways off,

"Hey...you are not gonna paddle off and leave me, are ya?"

We had caught a wave and had started down the other side when we caught a glimpse of Eepo trying to catch up. Randy found some paddles and handed one to me, and we started to back-paddle as hard as we could; we were closing the distance between Eepo and ourselves when Lucy touched my shoulder,

"Papa, look..." I turned my head over my left shoulder, and behind Eepo were several dorsal fins closing fast that were difficult to see because of the rising and falling of the sea and the color of the sky.

I looked at Randy, and he shook his head as he had already spotted them. We were within 10 yards of Eepo when Randy did the unimaginable: he stood up and dove over the side.

"Ah, crap! Here we go again!"

I was positive we had seen the last of Eepo and Randy at that point. I made my way to the other side of the raft, trying to keep it pointed towards the last place I had seen Randy hit the water, but the moving horizon and the herd of sharks kinda kept my attention.

The first shark wasn't any more than 15 feet from the raft when Eepo shot up over the gunnel, landed on his head and right shoulder, and gave out a groan,

"OH, SHIT!"

"Where's Randy?" I asked.

"I don't know! He just threw me into the boat!"

I made my way to the side and searched, and all of a sudden in the dark water, an even darker shade of liquid floated to the surface. I was sure it was blood, and the odds were it was Randy's blood at that.

Damn! I leaned back against the gunnel with my arm resting on the top when something grabbed my arm, and I thought I was dead!

I turned to see just how much of my right arm I was missing when Randy's head appeared,

"How about a boost, pard?"

"JESUS, you sure know how to make an entrance!" I said as I helped Randy over the side into the raft.

"That's a pretty nasty wound," I said as I laid him flat on the deck.

"Lucy, gal, would ya see if you can find a first aid kit?"

"It'll be in one of those boxes on the port side," Randy informed.

"Is that the first time you've been bitten by a shark?" I asked.

"No, but I hope it's the last! I think I'm about to run out of chances!"

His wounds were very deep across both sides of his right calf, and it took a tourniquet to stop the bleeding while I got a dressing on it.

"How the hell did you get away from those man-eaters?" I asked.

"I managed to hit the first one on the nose and then slit its throat, which started a feeding-frenzy, and I slipped away."

"You, my friend, are one hell of a man!" I said as we tried to regroup.

"What's next, Eepo?" I asked, and he looked at Randy for direction.

"There's a satellite phone in one of the boxes, but it won't do us any good until the sun comes up, and we can get it charged, so let's try and get some rest, so we can be on our toes in the morning."

We dined on dehydrated meat of some kind, which reminded me of that old Chinese saying, "When was the last time you ate cat, not counting, now?"

We also ate some cookies of some kind and drank water. I guess I should have been grateful, but you know how that goes.

"Hey, baby girl, you wouldn't happen to have a slug of Crown, would ya?"

"Yeah, babe, ya want to grab my purse?"

"Sure, where is it?" I asked.

She pointed down.

"I looked, "Down where?"

"Bout 1500 feet," and she started to laugh out loud. "Sometimes you are so easy," she said.

My heart sank.

At sunrise, I saw Randy's legs standing outside the shelter. He had a thin rope tied around the satellite phone and had it laying on the roof, absorbing the sunlight,

"Shouldn't take but 15 or 20 minutes to fully charge. Looks like we caught a swell that's moving us towards the shore," he said.

"How the hell do you know that?" I asked.

"I'm a sailor," he replied.

"I'm a sailor, too, and I don't have a clue where the hell we are!"

"Ok...the compass built into this phone doesn't hurt either," and we both laughed.

I heard Eepo moan and realized we had not bothered to check him out once we all got settled; his skin was on fire, and there was swelling around his gut when I lifted his shirt. Obviously, he had sustained some blunt-force trauma, most likely from the impact of the chopper hitting the ocean.

"Hey, Randy, I think Eepo is bleeding internally."

"Looks like it; they've been out looking for us all night long. I just gave HQ our coordinates, and they are not too far away."

"Thank GOD!"

The helo ride back to Oahu seemed like an eternity: every air pocket seemed to take my breath away, and for the first time, Lucy wasn't looking none to spry. I squeezed her hand, and she faked a smile. With the exception of a few scrapes and bruises as well as the bite, Randy didn't look that worse for the wear. Lord, I do believe love and youth are truly wasted on the young!

Hole 10

Two days later, Lucy and I were just checking out of the hospital when my new cell phone rang,

"Roc, here!"

"Roc, it's Eepo, how ya feelin, ol' friend?"

"Not too bad. We're just leaving the hospital."

"I know! Look straight ahead!"

I looked out the lobby doors, and Eepo and Randy were waving at us and behind them, an HSP helicopter was on the pad with its blades turning slowly.

"I'm surprised they let you guys check out another bird. You're pretty damn hard on equipment, if ya know what I mean?"

"Well, I guess they figure if we're gonna kill ourselves, they may as well get credit for it!" and we all laughed.

"And, I bet the powers that be are really gonna get nervous when we climb aboard that company jet and head for Japan."

"What's that?" I asked.

"I didn't stutter," Eepo replied, "We're headed for Japan if you're interested!"

I looked Lucy in the eye,

"Whaddaya think, kiddo?"

"Sign me up!"

There really wasn't any doubt in my mind as to what her answer might be, so about four hours later we were in the air headed for the coast of Japan. Normally, the flight takes about eight and a half hours by common carrier, but Eepo said we could make it in about five if we stayed in our seats and kept our mouths closed. Has it dawned on y'all that this old boy who really doesn't care for flying is doing one hell of a lot of it? Yeah, me too!

We deplaned at a private hanger at Tokyo International Airport looking like the *walking-wounded.*

Eepo was walking bent over, nursing the stitches in his abdomen, and Randy was walking with a cane, favoring the chunk that was bit out of his right leg. Lucy and I...well...we were just kinda beat all to hell in general. So, that walk down the stairway of our private jet to the tarmac looked like a good half mile straight down.

The eight-mile limo ride to the Tokyo Station Hotel was frightening in itself due to the amount of traffic and people moving in all directions like herds of cattle.

Eight miles took us a little over 40 minutes, and I had to wake Lucy from a pretty sound sleep when we arrived, and I was kinda relaxed myself, but then the magnificent facade of the huge entrance to the hotel came into view, and it was breathtaking.

"Lucy...get a look at this! I can't remember ever seeing anything so magnificent!" and she looked.

"Oh, my!" she gasped, "That is beautiful!"

We walked into the giant foyer of the hotel and headed towards the front desk that seemed a 100 yards away, and about halfway to our destination in a small seating area over to my right, something in my peripheral vision made my head spin.

I'll be damned! You know how I feel about coincidences, right? Well, there sat eight old and very well-dressed, prosperous-looking men with whom I had become reasonably well-acquainted, and at the back of the table, looking directly at me was my old friend, Trae Biggs, who was leaning back in his chair, all tanned and healthy with his sun glasses up on his blonde head. What the hell?

I pulled Lucy close to me; she could tell something was wrong, and I didn't want to talk about it, so we moved to the outside of Eepo and Randy, and I looked back when we were eight or ten steps ahead, and no one in the group seemed to look any more concerned at least, for the moment.

We rode one of the many elevators headed for the 42nd floor, and I spoke,

"Eepo, what do you suppose eight very wealthy men who were just in Hawaii to play golf would be doing in Japan?"

"Hypothetically speaking?" he asked.

"Sure, let's say that," I replied.

"Well, they could be here for a Kobe steak, the best in the world, or hell, Roc, I don't know!"

"And my friend, the pilot, was sitting with them all calm, looking like he just 'ate the canary.'"

"Roc, I'm starting to think this is a little more than hypothetical."

"Yeah, Eepo, they were all sitting in that area to our right as we came in. I don't believe they saw Lucy and I, but you never can tell."

"What do you think is goin on?"

"I'm not sure, but everybody winding up in Japan at the same time is way more than a coincidence," I said as my mind was reeling.

Papa Pau was in the Emperor's Suite, which was a cool $2500 a night and no golf, what a gyp!

He spoke to two of his bodyguards,

"You two stay well back but keep me in sight no matter where I go. I'm not expecting any trouble, but you never know." and they both acknowledged that they understood.

Trae Biggs turned a funny color of purple and red when he responded to the knock on his hotel room door and saw me standing there,

"Roc! What the hell are you doin here?"

"I could ask you the same question, my young friend!"

"Ah...I'm...ah...I'm…"

"Don't bother telling me any lies. I already have a rather good handle on what's going on. How deep in this mess are you, kiddo? Have you hauled or sold any drugs?" I asked as I studied his red face.

"Roc, I haven't done anything! They were just getting ready to bring me into the organization, but so far, I'm not involved at all!"

"I hope that's true because I'd hate to see you go down with these guys. You know as well as anyone how greed has brought more good men down than all the fancy women in the world. You need to stay in your room and don't answer yer phone unless it's me, do ya hear me?"

"Yes, sir...I hear ya!"

"Good! If ya don't want to spend the rest of yer life in prison, you better do exactly what I say, and we may get you out of this!"

"Maybe I can help you, Roc."

"How?" I asked.

"I don't know, but I feel like I should do something!"

"Right! Stay in your room! That's something!"

I walked down the hall towards the elevator and thought,

How did my young friend go from running a successful charter air service to a sniveling young kid in a couple of days? It seems that common sense is a plant that doesn't grow in everyone's garden.

Later on, we all met in the room where Eepo and Randy were staying, and I explained Trae's dilemma, while Eepo formulated a plan of attack,

"If Trae hasn't done anything but fly the chartered plane, he shouldn't have a problem."

"I suppose we'll see."

Like Eepo, I wasn't a hundred-percent sure about young Trae.

Eepo connected with his counterpart in the Japanese State Police, and we had a half a dozen plain-clothes officers huddling around us as Eepo, Randy, and their head guy put a plan into action.

Papa Pau and his crew were the ones we were there for and really didn't have any reason to arrest the other eight businessmen unless they gave us cause to do so, and I truly hoped they would!

As Lucy and I waited, my mind drifted back to a time when JJ and I were playing a round of golf with a set of twins who we had met in one of our favorite night spots on the San Diego Coast.

They said they had already made plans for the evening, so we set up a round of golf for the following day with everyone knowing full-well that it would end in a romantic interlude, and so it did! Almost!

We played nine holes of golf that were very uneventful then on to a quick and inexpensive dinner, and we ended up back at their apartment. We had a cocktail and some small talk, and then JJ and I headed off to two separate bedrooms and the heaven that waited beyond those doors; fortunately for JJ and me, we hadn't had time to get our Bermuda shorts much below our knees when this very masculine voice from the main room came booming,

"Honey...I'm home!"

"AH, CRAP!"

I pulled up my shorts, grabbed at and missed my flip-flops, bent over and kissed my date on the forehead who was lying naked, spread eagle on the king-size bed, and hurled myself through the bedroom window that just happened to be open.

As I was about three-quarters of the way out, I remembered we were on the second floor, and figured that the fall was going to be excruciating or at least the landing would be.

Should I land on my front or my back? Decisions, decisions, and the ground came barreling up at me, and then I knew it would be the front! I'm not sure what kind of plant or bush it was, but it was hearty enough to break my fall without breaking too many bones!

As I tried to extricate myself from a very difficult situation, I looked to my right and saw a pair of naked feet standing there.

Oh, Lord, I'm dead!

"Hey, pard, whaddya doin in the bushes?" JJ asked with a grin.

I pointed to the second-story window, then I asked,

"How'd you get out?" and he pointed to the small balcony just outside the other room's window.

"Besides, you were with that guy's wife, so I had a little more time."

"Did you know she was married?"

"Ah...yeah!"

"When were ya gonna let me know?" I asked.

"Probably never if we hadn't got caught, unless of course, you fell in love."

I had just barely gotten to my feet when gunshots rang out, and dirt flew all around us. JJ grabbed my hand, and we ran like hell!

A week or so later, officer Dan Brown came a knockin,

"Hey, sheriff, how ya doin?"

JJ and I had managed to put the beautiful twin incident behind us and out of our minds.

"Do you fellers know a set of twins who live over by the country club?"

"Yeah, they are cute girls. Why? What's up?" I asked, ready to tell him the whole funny story.

"They're saying you two broke in and tried to rape them!"

"They said what?"

Fortunately for us, Dan gave us the chance to explain our side,

"Tuesday night, we met them in the bar, and then people saw us together the next day for three hours or so, and we escaped another close call."

"Ya know," JJ said, "One of these days, it's all gonna catch up with us!"

"Yeah, but in the meantime, ain't it fun?" I said with a big smile.

Eepo yelled out the hotel room door,

"Ok, you all huddle up," and we gathered in the suite.

"Pau is settled down in the Emperor's Suite two floors up," Eepo said.

"The lieutenant, Mr. Reese, Ms. Barns, and I are goin to pay him a visit, while Sergeant Randall Jones and the rest of you cover the lobby and try and round up the old gentleman without making any more of a scene than necessary. We're gonna attempt to get them all in the conference room on the first floor; try to keep them separated as much as possible until we question them."

Everyone nodded their understanding, and Randy was the first to lead his group out the door.

I thought our floor was special, but the 45th floor was exquisite! Everything was gilded from the lamps to the ceiling as well as the frames that held some very special paintings that truly looked like the old masters had painted them. I certainly didn't have the expertise to know. All I knew was there was gold everywhere, almost to the point of being obscene, at least in my mind.

Lucy and I spread out: her behind the Japanese officer, and me behind Eepo; he knocked, and we waited, and it seemed like it took longer than five minutes for someone to answer the door of the Emperor's Suite; then the door lock rattled and slowly opened,

"Yes?"

"It's the manager, and I need a word with Mr. Pau."

The bodyguard turned, and Eepo put a gun to his back and pushed him into the room, and we followed.

Papa Pau had papers spread out all over the giant bed that had to be at least a king and a half! I mean it was huge! He was lying on his back, talking on the phone with his eyes closed. When he looked up, he couldn't believe his eyes,

"What the hell are you doing here?" he shouted with fire in his eyes.

"Shoot these damn people!" he screamed, but none of his bodyguards moved.

"Oh, hell...I'll do it myself!" and he reached under his pillow and came out with an automatic handgun, and no one else seemed to be paying any attention to Papa Pau.

However, I could see that he was really going to shoot someone, so I pulled the slide on my Glock 19 and put a round in each of his knees, and he screamed while at the same time, his gun discharged into the top of the canopy bed, then on into the ceiling, and then the gun fell to the bed in silence.

"You son of a bitch! You shot me! I'll kill you, ya bastard!"

"I'll keep an eye out for ya," I said with a smirk.

"I'm sure I'll be dead long before you get out of prison, *POP!*" and I could see the fire in his eyes underneath the pain.

By the time I got downstairs, Randy had the old geezers rounded up and separated in the very large conference room, and they were looking hard at each other, trying to figure out what story they were going to tell until Lucy and I walked into the room, and they all turned a special color of pale.

"Gentlemen...what a coincidence all you being here in this beautiful hotel at the same time! By the way, I don't know if any of you are acquainted with the importer, Mr. Pau, but he is under arrest and has a couple of bullets in his scrawny body, so if any of you had meetings scheduled with him, he won't be available for oh...I'd say about 50 years!"

Every one of the old geezers turned an even deeper red and looked at one another, trying to figure out what just happened.

Eepo and Lucy stood on either side while I rambled on, and they seemed to truly be enjoying my recitation, so, I continued,

"Your ride back to Hawaii, I'm not really sorry to say, won't be quite as comfortable as the one coming over as common air lines don't have quite the amenities you're used to, but then, the rest of yer lives are all gonna be a little different by the time this is over, so just sit back and prepare to be humiliated."

They all swallowed hard, and a few had tears running down their cheeks.

Eighteen hours passed since we touched down in Tokyo, and we had collected our prize, Papa Pau, and with the help of some of Eepo's friends in the Japan State Police, we managed to get the eight financial giants out of the country without too much paperwork as the Japanese really didn't want to get involved.

We loaded Mr. Pau on board Trae's Lear jet, and Lucy, Eepo, Randy, and I headed off into the sky like a bullet. Damn...what a way to travel!

Hole 11

When we got back to Hawaii, Lucy and I decided to take a couple of days to relax and play some golf before we returned home to San Diego. Our bruises were all just about healed, and we both needed the fresh air

The pro at the hotel golf course tried to pair us with another couple, but we begged off, saying we were beginners and just wanted to play at our own pace and promised not to hold anyone up. We teed off and were gone, never to be seen again.

We were on the Par 3, 16th green just taking in the beautiful Ocean and surroundings when the flagstick snapped in half, and four holes appeared within inches of our feet.

"Get to the cart! Run!" I yelled, and we both sprinted the 30 yards, or so, back to our golf cart. Once there, I unzipped the pocket of the front of my golf bag that held my wallet, watch, and my Glock 19 and pumped a round into the chamber, and Lucy retrieved hers, and we huddled beside the colorful golf cart and waited for the next round of bullets.

I didn't have Eepo's number saved in my cell, so I had to scroll down the "last called" list, and his was about 20 numbers down, but finally, his voicemail came on,

"This is Lieutenant Russel Eepo, I'm on another call at the moment; please leave a message, and I'll return your call as soon as possible. Thank you…BEEP!"

"Eepo…it's Roc…someone is shooting at us and has us pinned down on the 16th green here at the hotel golf course!"

I was just getting ready to try and find Randy's number when my phone rang,

"Yeah!" I said.

"Roc…it's Eepo! I'm on my way, about five minutes out!"

"Someone has an automatic rifle with a suppressor because we didn't hear a thing, so we don't have a clue where he is!"

"Just hang tight, Roc. I'm messaging Randy as we speak," and the line went dead.

For some reason that sounded a little different this time, *dead!*

A few minutes later, Eepo showed up,

"I thought you had this thing all wrapped up!"

"Well, Roc, all the major players are in the *pokey*."

"Well, then, who the hell is shootin at us?" I asked.

"I haven't got a clue, but one thing's for sure, they are not very proficient when it comes to using an automatic rifle because the shots had to come from over the hill by the clubhouse, and it's not that far away. So either they're a really bad shot, or they were not tryin to hit you."

That made me think.

Randy pulled up on a motorcycle just as we were getting ready to leave the 16th green,

"Meet me at the pro shop," I said, and Lucy and I headed up the hill.

"Do you have a member named *David Pau?*" I asked the pro at the counter.

"No, sir, but he plays here from time to time; he's comped, has *friends in high places,* if you know what I mean?"

"Yeah, I think I do; when was the last time he was here?"

The pro had a peculiar look on his face, like *are you kidding?*

"Why, he just left about 10 minutes ago. He arrived about an hour and a half ago, picked up a cart and a large bucket of balls, and went to the practice facilities."

"Do you know what kind of car he drives?" I asked.

"Yes, a newer-model Jeep, orange...bright-orange!"

"Eepo, can you find out if our friend, David, has another residence and put an BOLO out on his vehicle?"

"Already workin on it, Roc. Let's head for the parking lot."

"Where are we going, love?" Lucy asked with some concern in her voice.

"I have a feeling our friend, David, is very familiar with the Pau Ranch!"

Just then my phone rang,

"Yeah, Eepo, what is it?"

"The Ranch address is what he has listed as his home address."

"That's what I thought," I said. "Headed that way."

"Let Randy and I get ahead of you."

"You better hurry, then," I said, as Randy blew by us on the left.

I was going 70, and he must have been doing over a 100, like we were standing still.

"So much for Randy; where are you?"

"Coming up on your tail," and I saw the red and blue lights in my rearview mirror, and a few seconds later, Eepo flashed by us on our left as well.

I accelerated to a manageable speed, then powered onto the road of the Pau farm, or ranch, or pineapple orchard, or whatever.

As we approached the main house, I saw Randy's bike down in the parking area with Randy underneath, not moving, and Eepo's SUV up on the porch of the main house, slammed through the front door. The driver's door was open, and Eepo was hanging out, also not moving. I pulled the big Mercedes hard to the right just as a high-powered round came through the center of the windshield,

"KEEP YER HEAD DOWN, GIRL!" I yelled as the back tires broke loose, and we spun hard in a semi-circle and then shot off towards the right side of the guest house.

"What's your plan, papa?"

"Right now, I'm just tryin to keep us alive. I'm sure he's in the guesthouse. Please stay in the car until this is over!"

"Yes, dear!"

Crap, I knew that tone, but I didn't have time to argue. We power-slid to a stop with sand and rocks flying in all directions, and I slid out low and made my way towards the side of the cottage and to the front, just as five or six bullets riddled the windshield, causing it to collapse inward. I felt cold chills all over and could only hope that Lucy was ok.

I moved even faster to the corner of the house, then across the front under the big bay window and up to the front door. It was ajar, so I crawled in and slithered down the hall as cautiously as possible. I made my way around the corner behind the large sofa, and then a voice came from behind me,

"Don't move, Mr. Reese."

I felt something very cold and hard against the back of my head.

"Turn around, slowly! Push yer gun over here," and I did as I was told (something I wasn't accustomed to doing, and it really pissed me off!).

"I tried to warn you off, Mr. Reese; why didn't you just go home?"

"I don't know, just something about being shot at that kinda makes me mad, I guess."

"Well, you will really be upset when I put a half-dozen bullets in yer chest," and he raised the barrel of the automatic rifle a couple of inches.

"Ya, know, David, I've had a pretty good life, and if this is where it ends, then I guess that's that, but can you tell me why you were shooting at us in the first place?"

"My Uncle Pau gave me orders to kill you, but I couldn't make myself do it. Now things have changed, and I'm not going to prison!"

"You are right about that!" and as his finger moved toward the trigger guard, his head exploded.

Blood, bone, and brain matter covered my face, so I didn't see him fall to the floor. My hands were a bloody mess from trying to clear my eyes, and when I was able to focus, I saw a blurred vision of Lucy standing there with a smoking gun, still pointing at the spot where David was standing a short second or two earlier.

"Are you two alright?" Eepo yelled as he burst into the room with a gun flailing in his right hand and blood oozing from his left shoulder. Randy was right behind him with a gouge above his right eye and several bloody scrapes over his arms and bare legs.

"We're fine, but good ol' David didn't fare quite so well!"

"I should have known," Eepo replied, shaking his head.

We sat on the patio of the guest house overlooking the Pacific and partaking of a giant Crown Reserve on the rocks as the crime scene crew went through the house and gathered evidence for their case. Lucy set the gallon bottle of Crown down in the middle of the table before the crew could take it.

"So, Roc, did David say why he needed to kill you?" Eepo asked.

"He said that Papa Pau had instructed him to take me out, but after the event at the hotel, he couldn't bring himself to do it. When he saw you and Randy, he knew he was toast, and he had no intention of going to prison."

"All that money and in line as the next royalty of the islands, and he ended up as just a pile on the floor; what a waste!" Eepo said, and we all agreed and took a very large pull on our tumblers.

Hole 12

We had been airborne for about 45 minutes when the copilot came and advised me that Captain Trae would like a word with me.

"Roc, have a seat," and I settled down into the very comfortable, second in command's bucket seat.

"I don't know how to say just how grateful I am. If you hadn't been there, my life would have been over."

"Yeah, kiddo, it truly would have been, and you need to keep focused on what you have and realize that lots of money doesn't mean a thing if you have to keep worrying about who's going to take it from ya. You are in a great position and are able to travel the world as you please."

"I know, Roc; it won't happen again, and of course, you and Lucy are my heroes, and I am in your debt from now on. Anything you need, anywhere in the world you want to go, anytime, just say the word!"

"What was that all about?" Lucy asked.

"Just young Trae expressing his gratitude."

"Can I freshen your drink, Mr. Reese?" the beautiful hostess asked as we hurled through the sky at breakneck speed.

Epilogue

We had been back in San Diego two days, and Lucy and I were itching to get to the golf course and let off some frustration. There is just something about hitting a golf ball in the mouth and feeling it fly off the club face with ease and sail on a perfect line that is like nothing else.

If yer not a golfer, let me see if I can come close to explaining the feeling: it's like...ah...nope...I don't believe I have the ability or the words to explain that feeling.

Lucy was out doing some *rat-killing*, and JJ had fixed the two of us up with a couple of restaurateurs who owned three very exclusive joints on the Coast who considered themselves pretty good *sticks* and had wanted to play us for many months.

JJ had been putting them off just to keep them chomping at the bit, and when they finally got the call, they could hardly wait to get play, too bad for them!

We were on the third hole, and they had pushed the first and won the second.

"Hey...you guys wanna kick it up a few bucks, say like a grand and press when yer pissed?"

Sometimes $500 a hole just doesn't get yer blood rushing.

JJ looked at me with that grin that I have grown so used to, and I just winked back,

"If that will make you happy, why not?" he said.

We won the third, and they pressed, pushed the fourth, won the fifth, and they pressed, pushed the sixth and seventh, and they thought they saw a chink in our armor. Then JJ and I both birdied the eighth and ninth to each win $4500 on the front, and I thought our opponents were going to cry as their faces were blood-red as they headed for the clubhouse to get some adult beverages like that would make a difference!

"So, what exactly happened over in Hawaii?" JJ asked.

"Well, that nice old couple known as the Paus ended up being the biggest drug importers and exporters between the U.S. and Japan, and they were behind the murder of their son; then old man Pau killed his wife, and do you want to hear any more?"

"Oh, hell no! That's more than enough for me! Let's just play some nice, quiet golf and try not to get shot!"

We gave our opponents the opportunity to lower the bet on the back side, but that would have caused them to lose face, and we knew they wouldn't accept anyway, but they still thought they could beat us.

Another five grand on the back side, and we bought drinks at the Men's Grill and believe me, they took advantage of our generosity: they staggered to their cars, talking about a rematch and how we were just incredibly lucky that day, yeah right!

Later that afternoon around 4, Lucy and I took the two-man kayak out and did our regular four miles, then grilled some large, custom-cut filets on the grill with some fresh asparagus, a Caesar salad, and a bottle of very nice Merlot (I was kinda getting to like the wine thing) and then a very large Crown Royal Reserve on the rocks, and we watched the sun go all the way down, and life was good.

THE END...at least for now.

Join Roc and Lucy on their next adventure as they travel to paradise in...

Birdies & Costa Rica Heat

coming soon!!

For book signings and speaking engagements, contact Duke at

DukeCharlesWriter@gmail.com

Like Duke on Facebook

Follow Duke on LinkedIn

O<small>THER</small> B<small>OOKS BY</small> D<small>UKE</small> C<small>HARLES</small>

LUKE KASH WESTERN SERIES

People of the Horse
Spirit and the Blood
Blood and Thunder
Thunder Cloud and Spirit Walker

ROC REESE MYSTERY SERIES

Birdies and San Diego Heat
Birdies and Vegas Heat
Birdies and Texas Riviera Heat
Birdies and Costa Rica Heat

LEROY LOVELADY SERIES
A Texas Melody
The Texas Two-Step

OTHER BOOKS BY DUKE

Duke Charles' Shorts
Blanco River Wars
Black Wolf Moon
4 Steps Back to Here
Fire on the Water

To find out more about Duke Charles, visit his website

at

DukeCharles.com